I0581453

# LIGHTLY FANTASTICAL

FICTION BY
*Jemma Dyer*
*Avery Miskin*
*McKelle Snedaker*

EDITED BY
*Peter and Jeanne Anderson*

PUBLISHED BY
*House on a Road Books*

2021

Book design and typography by Meggan Laxalt Mackey, Studio M Publications & Design, Boise, Idaho.

Art by Publitek dba GoGraph.

Library of Congress Cataloging-in-Publication Data
     *Lightly Fantastical: An Anthology of Short Fiction.*

Summary:
     *Lightly Fantastical* is a product of participants in
     Book Publishing, a short course offered to students
     of Teton Middle School, Driggs, Idaho, during the
     winter term, 2021.

Published by House on a Road Books, Teton Valley, Idaho

FIRST EDITION
ISBN 978-1-7342192-2-7

# LIGHTLY FANTASTICAL

*The best fantasy is written in the language of dreams.*
*It is alive as dreams are alive, more real than real…*
*for a moment at least…*
*that long magic moment before we wake.*


George R. R. Martin

# CONTENTS

# INTRODUCTION

An experienced reader and writer enjoys no finer privilege,
I believe, than encouraging the love of reading and writing
in burgeoning intellectual souls, by which of course I mean
young people. How young varies. Some young people—
including the three featured in this collection—are already
deep in the process of devouring the writing of other
authors, digesting and synthesizing that material within
their own imaginations and then producing their own
creative literary outputs, perhaps almost as relief valves
for the pressures building within them.

All three of our contributors acknowledge consuming
piles of books, probably reading novels when they should
be doing other things, a form of misconduct I too relished
from middle-school through today. Although having very
different personalities and coming from widely varying
backgrounds, the three of them share the tendency to want
to write, to ache to write. Accordingly, they write constantly.

It took me a while longer than Avery, McKelle and
Jemma. My first published short story I created when
I was 15 years old. These writers are out of the gate faster
than I was.

Wallace Stegner famously spoke of the long apprentice-
ship for young writers. He pointed to the facts that writing
is an inordinately difficult undertaking, cannot readily be
taught and only produces good results for a few individual
writers, usually by surprise, after they have traversed years
of drudgery and mounting disappointments. What young
writers need, Stegner observes, is an environment in which
to write. Since writing students learn best from each other,
an environment conducive to sharpening writing skills is
one in which writers can congregate and share. This little
anthology, the product of a brief class on book publishing,
is intended to offer exactly that sort of environment.

Creative writing opens windows into the accumulated experiences of the individual writer. The best stories are usually those that bespeak lives deeply-lived by their authors. Flaubert once commented that a writer should be able to distinguish one cart horse from all other cart horses. In other words, writing is only something that can happen after a lifetime of careful observation of minute detail in the surrounding world. But Henry James doubted that advice, instead suggesting, in typically Jamesian fashion, that a writer should be someone upon whom nothing is lost.

I tend to agree with Henry James on that. Although life experience and detailed observation of the world takes time to develop, it is a mistake to think that young writers don't already have depth and the ability to see and understand. The contributors to *Lightly Fantastical*, a title suggested by Jemma Dyer, by the way, are most certainly young writers upon whom nothing is lost.

In the broader literary sense, the stories included in this collection would qualify as what is called juvenilia. This is not an insult to our contributors. The term implies early experiments by highly-talented individuals with their creative processes. I am very confident that each of these writers has the skill and drive to take their writing wherever they wish in the years ahead. We will see great things coming from each of them. But for now, it's highly enjoyable to peek into their imaginations and discover elements of their hopes and despairs, sureties and anxieties, confidences and knee-knocking self-doubts. This is the organic material of which literature is made.

I thank Avery, McKelle and Jemma for sharing their time and their creative worlds with us in the Spring of 2021 and beyond.

—*Peter Anderson*

# JEMMA
## DYER

# DEATHBELL COMMAND

We were zooming through space towards Earth in the ELM (Earth Landing Mechanism). No one had been there for over 200 years because of the deathbell plague. We weren't going to return to Earth ever again -- at least not until our population increased and the B3LL had trouble sustaining it.

Our team was being sent to Earth because the government decided we were the most useless team ever. They sent us to a disease-ridden planet as guinea pigs to see if the air was breathable and the world livable again. I was in a team of six women: Sam the captain, Isabelle the mechanic, Lilly the doctor, Mary the botanist, Ally the epidemiologist, and me, Mira the genius strategist.

"Entering Earth atmosphere," A robotic voice said while the words flashed across a screen in front of me.

"Well, everyone should sit down, I guess," Sam said as she pulled on her straps to ensure their tightness. I strapped myself into my chair and held onto the handles on either side of me as we gained speed to an exhilarating pace heading straight down to Earth. Soon we slowed and bounced to a soft stop on an old dried-up field.

"Uhh, what should we do now," Isabelle asked as we all unstrapped ourselves.

"We should go out and get to work," Sam said as if it was obvious.

"No," Ally said blocking the door. "We should let me get my gear out and test the air so there isn't a possibility of us all dying immediately when we step outside."

"Yeah, we should probably do that first," Sam said, slowly turning around and walking away from the door.

Once Ally had tested the air and confirmed that there were only small traces of the Plague and it was not enough to affect us in any way, we stepped out onto the surface of Earth.

"According to my maps, we're somewhere called California," I said, looking at a map of the United States. "Its average temperature is 110 degrees Fahrenheit."

"Well, that explains the heat but not the flowers," Mary said looking around. Only then did I notice the tons of flowers surrounding us. They were a deep purple and had little bell-shaped purple bulbs covering the entire flower.

"Nobody touches any of these flowers until I have a chance to check them out," Mary said, pulling on a glove and picking one of the flowers.

We all started unpacking the ELM and setting it up as a semi-permanent living structure. Well, everyone but Mary; she was performing tests on the flowers we had found earlier. Once we were done setting up the ELM as a living structure, we took out six of the individual meal packets and ate our dinner.

The next morning Mary had the results on the tests from the night before.

"The flowers are completely safe for humans, but they're not safe for human consumption," Mary told us once we had all gathered for breakfast in the morning. "Don't eat them."

◎◎◎

We had been on Earth for eight days and I was liking it. Even though it was super-hot, it was also way quieter than it was on the B3LL and we found there is way more water on Earth. At least it was good until Mary started acting weird. She would eat her whole day's rations in one meal and then wouldn't eat for days. We all worried about her even though she claimed she felt fine. We could all hear her coughing non-stop every night. Then one night we didn't hear her coughing. The next morning, we all feared the worst, but when we got up, Mary was already up and looking much better than previous days. She had even spruced up the ELM with some of the flowers from the field outside.

"Uh, so why are you up so early," Isabelle asked Mary as she started heading towards the door.

"The early bird gets the worm," Mary said in a chipper tone none of us had ever heard her use.

"Yeah, but you hate the morning," Sam said.

"Well, not anymore.  I thought about it and realized that the more I'm awake the more I can get done."

"None of this sounds like the Mary we know," Lilly whispered to me.

"Yeah, definitely not," I whispered back. Ally walked over and picked up one of the flowers to smell it.

"Ewww," Ally said, "this smells disgusting. Why would you bring this into the house, Mary?"

"I quite like how they smell and how they look," Mary said curtly.

That night, while we were going to sleep, I heard someone get out of their sleeping bag and walk over to the living room space. I got up to see who it was, and what they were doing, and what I saw stunned me. Mary was sitting on the ground with a pile of the purple flowers next to her. Her hands and mouth were painted purple and she was unmoving on the ground.

Mary was dead and I finally realized what the flowers were called. They were the deathbells the plague was named after. I stumbled back to the sleeping area and fell to the floor sobbing.

I knew none of us were safe from the grip of the deathbells, but I did know one thing. Ally was next. I also was pretty sure that nobody could stop what was going to happen to us. As I slowly lost consciousness, I heard a deep throaty cough coming from the corner where Ally slept.

◎◎◎

I woke to the sounds of sobbing and Sam leaning over me with a concerned look on her face.

"Thank god you're awake," Sam said. "What's going on?" I didn't know what she meant for a second but then what I saw last night came rushing back to me.

"I know why the plague is called the Deathbell now," I said. "The flowers are the Deathbells, and the flowers surrounding us are what killed 99.99 percent of Earth's population. There's no way to stop what's going to happen, but Ally is the next victim of the Deathbell."

"What!?!?" Sam yelled. Once we were all gathered near Mary's dead body, I explained everything.

"Let me get this straight," Isabelle said standing up. "We're surrounded by the diseased flowers that almost wiped out all of humanity. You get the disease by touching the flower and the poison from the bells takes over your brain and makes you eat the flowers till it kills you."

"Yeah, pretty much," I said, "and I saw Ally touching one of the flowers yesterday. Plus I heard her coughing last night."

"Oh no, oh no, we're all doomed aren't we," Lilly said quietly as she started rocking back and forth.

"No, we just have to get off this planet as soon as possible," Sam said.

"Uh, slight problem with that," Isabelle started.

"What now," Sam said, getting angrier by the second.

"Someone sabotaged the engine," Isabelle said, scooting back to give Sam some space.

"Who was it?" Sam said with a growl hidden behind her words and an accusing glare on her face.

"Probably Mary," Isabelle said frankly, "and for the record even if I work around the clock, it could take me up to a month to fix the engine, and even then, it still might not ever work." Sam then got up and started pacing in furious circles.

"What do you mean it might not ever work again?" Sam yelled.

"I mean that Mary smashed the engine repeatedly with a sledgehammer and I might not be able to fix it," Isabelle said, getting exasperated.

"Anyway, we have to decide what to do with Ally," I said, bringing us back to the topic at hand. "She could infect all of us, and we all know she'll die in the next couple of days."

"But Is it ethically correct to just throw her out?" Lilly said timidly.

"You guys are the worst. You're all talking about me like I'm not here," Ally said, "I know you think I'll start eating them in the next couple of days, but I know I can resist the urge."

"Ok, we'll trust you but if you show any signs of attraction towards the deathbells we're going to throw you out," Sam said.

"I promise I won't," Ally said.

⊚⊚⊚

Two mornings later, we found Ally laying with Mary in her pile of deathbells. There were only four of us left now and anyone who touched a deathbell had to go.

⊚⊚⊚

"We've been here for three months now, and you still haven't made any actual progress on the engine. What have you been doing?!?!" Sam had been yelling a lot lately, mostly at Isabelle about the engine repairs. And I mean a lot. We hadn't gone outside once since Ally had died and we were all going a bit stir-crazy. Some more than others. I was doing pretty well with it, but now that the rain was coming in, we were about to go out again.

As we walked out of the door, Sam stepped in a puddle of water. We thought nothing of it until Lilly saw there was a deathbell floating in the water. The flower brushed against the exposed skin on Sam's ankle.

19

We all scrambled to get inside; Sam, so she wouldn't get thrown out, and me, Lilly, and Isabelle to lock Sam out. We won and that night we could hear a light sobbing and heavy coughing coming from right outside the door. Three days later we found her in the field of flowers, hands and face painted purple. Three were dead and we wouldn't be getting off Earth anytime soon.

◎◎◎

Four months later the engine was fixed but Isabelle was sitting with Sam in the field, her hands and face painted purple.

The four women were decaying but at least Lily and I had survived and were packing up the ELM back into a ship. I had been studying the manuals about how to fly the ship, and I felt ready.

That night we took off, set it on course and slept. As I was going to sleep, I heard a thick throaty cough coming from the other room.

Lilly must have been infected before we left, and I could only assume she had brought some to infect me too.

The next morning, I felt as if there was a constant war going on in my mind and by the end of the day the death-bells had won.

I felt like I could hear what Lilly was thinking. I took another hour or two to get back to the B3LL and no one greeted us when we got back. We assumed everyone was asleep.

We snuck to the half-filled reservoir in the back of the ship and dropped the extra flowers we had brought into it. We started slurping the water as fast as possible and were dead by the time the human race was wiped out for good.

# THE BURNING

As she saw her mother's skin melting off her face and falling into the flames below, as she heard her mother's screams mixed with her own—she was changed that night. The burning was happening again.

Out of all the women in the world who could have been accused of witchcraft, it was her mother. The most horrible thing about it was that her father was the one who had accused her. He had turned his own wife in. The mother of his child. . . for trying to save her only daughter.

Emily Evergreen was saving her daughter's life with medicine when her husband got home. He walked in and saw her, his smile dissipated, and he ran out. Her mother was sentenced to the burning and so started the career of one of the best witch hunters the world had ever seen.

Seven years later, I, 12-year-old Abigail Evergreen, was obsessed with bringing my mother back. After these years of trying, I was convinced that magic, the very thing that my mother was killed for, was the only thing that could do it. I had run away from home a mere month after my mother was killed. I had at least found a friend, another girl whose mother had been a victim of the burning. Her name was Charlotte Leenal. We had been learning necromancy together, and tonight was what it had all been leading up to.

At midnight Charlotte and I stood in front of the boxes that held our mothers' ashes mixed with the ashes of the fires that had consumed them. We opened the boxes and a giant midnight blue book with intricate silver lettering. We had been studying since we found it four years back. It was the ultimate guide to necromancy. It was opened to a page devoted to one line.

*Askinen meremestal etal ilkensh charalant*

Charlotte and I chanted. It was supposed to raise the dead from ashes, and we were really hoping it would work. We had tried all the other options. It was our only chance left and we had to accept that if this didn't work, we would have to give up.

The ashes stirred, as if starting to awaken.

"We have to say it again!" Charlotte screeched happily, it being the first breakthrough we had ever had.

*Askinen meremestal etal ilkensh charalant*

Then we saw a group of men standing in the doorway.

"WITCHES!" yelled a man I knew very well who seemed to be the leader of a group.

"Father!" I spat astonished and angry. Then the ashes stopped moving.

"Wind," Charlotte sighed, defeated.

"Get them," my father said with a growl hidden behind his words.

"Why do you want to kill me, Father?"

"Because I don't trust people who are witches or who are witches spawn," my father said as he lunged at us. "RUN," I mouthed at Charlotte. A second later we started running, but sadly we underestimated the men. After years of witch-hunting, they were way faster than us and overtook us in less than a minute.

After they caught us, they dragged us to the burning stake. They tied me to the stake first and started the fire.

It hurt like you can't imagine. Like if you've ever touched a kettle filled with boiling water or a cast iron pot full of stew. Then I felt it.

I felt the skin melting off my legs, then my stomach, then my chest and arms, and eventually my face. I screamed over and over as the skin on my body turned to ashes below me.

Some people can describe taking their last breath in stories, but I wasn't able to, because there was so much smoke billowing into my face and throat.

Right before my death, I felt someone come close to me. As soon as he spoke, I knew who it was.

"I'm sorry," my dad whispered as I fell into the obliviousness of death.

# AVERY
## MISKIN

# INTO THE PORTAL, AND OUT AGAIN

I didn't have to do English this year on account of my incredible vocabulary. My vocabulary is more advanced than some of the teachers' so even if I'm calling their class boring, they still say, "I totally felt what you felt while reading your poem." Enough about vocabulary, the point is I have a free period, which I usually spend in the Music room when I don't have work to do, but this time I decided to head to the library.

I opened the door and my eyes brought me to the library. The shelves were lined up in straight lines, just like always, but the seating arrangements were different and the posters on the walls had changed yet again. I made my way over to the librarian's desk in the corner checking the shelves along the way for good books.

"Do you have any other mysteries? I finished the others." She stared at me in surprise. As I said I'm not usually in the library at this time.

"No, not at the moment. But I did, uh, order some new ones just for you," she whispered. I grabbed a random book off the shelf behind me and settled into a chair to find out about the history of pirating. A voice came over the intercom, "Rel Dezago, please come to the office to retrieve your English lesson." As I said I have a free period but that didn't mean that my grandparents would let me always have it to myself. I pulled myself off the chair and slid the book back onto the shelf.

I made my way to the office which was on the other side of the school. When I finally got to the office the secretary glanced up at me and handed me the folder. "What took so long?" she asked.

"Library," I answered shortly. She nodded. I walked away clutching the folder which was overflowing with paper.

I made my way back to the library, surprisingly not dropping the folder. I turned the last corner and slammed into the History teacher. The papers flew everywhere. She looked me up and down, as if assessing if it was really worth it to get me in trouble. She walked away shaking her head and mumbling.

I hurriedly gathered the papers up and shoved them back into the folder. I walked into the library yet again. The librarian glanced up. She smiled. I sat down at a table and opened the folder. The first page on both sides said, "Pay close attention to all of this, skip nothing." I sighed knowing this would be a long lesson. I pulled the pages off the top and tossed them to the side. I then pulled out the rest of the paper and looked it over. French had three pages to complete while all the others had six. Oh, did I not mention that my vocabulary is only absolutely amazing in languages that aren't English. I am decent at English but I'm better at others.

I flipped to the back for the fun stuff, and by that, I mean the languages with figures, like Chinese. But my absolute favorite is probably Glanician, which is an amazing dead language. I set to work, drawing all the different characters to make a story. After what seemed like minutes, the bell rang. I glanced up. The papers were spread all over the table, I quickly gathered them up and stuffed them into the folder. I had gotten a lot done.

I went to find my backpack. I found that I had thrown it in the lunchroom. I grabbed it and hurried to my last class. I entered the classroom and prepared myself for another boring lesson. The class dragged by and after what seemed like five hours the bell rang, signaling the end of school.

I pushed my way through the other students and finally made it outside and to my grandparents' car. I opened the door and dropped into the seat. My grandma held out her hand for the folder.

She flipped through it as my grandpa started the car. "You actually got a lot done unlike most of the time. But Rel, you should pay more attention to your Delsh. You will need it one day."

"Why would I need it? It's a dead language."

"Not as dead as you think. Do we need to show you why?" I nodded. My grandpa pulled off the road. Then got out of the car and pulled me along. When we went through a hedge, I saw a pulsing purple glow.

"This is why you need to learn it well." I cocked my head to the side. "This is the barrier to Ramas, an evil place, and over there...," he said pointing, "...is the entrance to Elysia. We are keepers of this portal, and you will have to be as well."

A million thoughts raced through my head at that moment. Magic? Portals? What in the world is Ramas? Why is there a barrier over it?

I must have looked agitated because my grandma, who I didn't know had followed us, grabbed my shoulders, turned me around and gave me that "calm down" look. She pulled me away and put me back in the car. We drove away. When we got home, they explained why Ramas had a barrier.

"To protect the other worlds," my grandma said. I went to sleep with a feeling of trepidation. I woke up and looked out the window. Bright and sunny, a little windy by the looks of the trees but otherwise great. I went downstairs to find some breakfast. I found a note on the table that said, "Off to keep up the barrier. Be back in two hours. Love you."

I grabbed some cereal and sat down on the porch to wait for my grandparents to return. I waited for four hours then decided to find them. I remembered pretty well the route to the portals, so I walked. When I got there, I found a dragon pacing through the trees. He looked pretty content. Then I saw my grandma's purse lying on the ground and my grandpa's cane laying five feet from that. I realized that the dragon had eaten my grandparents. I got mad. I mean, really mad. I charged the dragon, only to come to knifepoint with an elf.

"You will only get hurt. I am bringing him back to Elysia. I am sorry about your grandparents! But you must keep up the barrier or everything as you know it will be gone," the elf said but not in English obviously, in Ulat, which is another language I learned. He backed away and guided the dragon into Elysia. I was surprised. I walked back home to ponder what to do.

I had wandered around my house for hours when I came upon my grandpa's journal. I opened it, unlike many journals which are about one's day, this was about the barrier and many other things. I read through and realized that I had been learning magic for years in my most neglected language, Delsh. My grandparents had been teaching me magic without me knowing it.

I read further. It talked about how often to keep up the barrier and the person inside, Jack. Jack had blown up an entire world. "That's what he meant, everything will be gone," I thought. I decided to investigate whether my grandparents had fixed the barrier.

The clearing was very similar to how it was before. I grabbed my grandma's purse and grandpa's cane I had left there previously. I looked up. The purple glow still emanated from the barrier but weaker than before. When I looked through the purple, I was surprised to see that I could see into Ramas. A silhouette walked around, the only moving thing in sight. They came close to the barrier.

"Have you come to put up the thing that keeps me trapped here, Alexander," the silhouette said vilely. My grandfather's name. I crept closer. The silhouette was a boy. A boy not much older than me. He jumped back. "Who are you?," he asked, sounding slightly frightened.

"Oh did you not see my grandfather get eaten by that dragon," I spat back.

"Your grandfather? That man is older than I thought," his voice softened, "Are you going to let me out?"

I shook my head.

"I'm going to keep you here." I pulled the journal out of my pocket and read the enchantment. This continued for a year, the conversation not differing much from:

"Back again, Rel?"

"Yes, I have to keep you here."

"You sure you don't want to let me leave?"

"Yes."

"See you next time."

"Probably."

Another day, I came once again to put up the barrier. The conversation differed a little bit.

"I wish you were a good person so I wouldn't have to do this," I said annoyed.

"Well actually you don't have to, you just do," he said. I glared at him. He glared back. "I'm serious, if you just didn't do it anymore you wouldn't have to come here three times a week and I could be free. I mean if it wasn't for your grandparents, I wouldn't be here in the first place, but oh well."

I finished the enchantment and stomped off. I had tried not to think about my grandparents much, it hurt a lot. But Jack had made it hurt worse.

I was consumed in grief, but I didn't do anything. The pain now was worse than the first time. The first time I at least remembered my responsibility. The next time I needed to put up the barrier it passed me by. I didn't realize it until too late.

I ran over to the barrier to find it gone and footprints in the mud leading to Elysia. I groaned. But not wanting to follow Jack, I headed home. I came upon my grandpa's journal once again. I began reading it but stopped when I came to the line that said, "Fifteen years of hard work…" Jack had wiped out a universe at the age of two. I gasped. At two?

Well, he'll be a lot more dangerous now. I left to go find him in Elysia.

I walked through the portal and was amazed. It was like Earth but absolutely picturesque everywhere I looked. I began wandering around wondering what to do. As I was gazing around, I bumped into someone.

"Ooh my goodness. Are you okay? By the way, I'm fine. OH MY GOODNESS. You're a human. We haven't had one in years," the boy said freaking out a bit. He had wings and was flitting around, so I guessed he was a fairy.

"I'm fine. I would ask you a question but based on your reaction to me, I don't think you will be able to answer it."

"You should ask anyway, you never know… also where did you learn Glanician? Your pronunciation is better than some native speakers."

I had not realized that I had spoken in Glancian because it came almost naturally to switch between languages.

"I learned from my grandparents, although they used to say that my pronunciation is terrible. I was going to ask if you've seen a dark-haired boy with green or blue eyes that is three or four inches taller than me."

"Sadly, I haven't seen that particular person but I do know who will." He grabbed my arm and dragged me across a few cornfields and what seemed like a bajillion rivers. I have never been so wet in my entire life. I was panting. He looked back.

"Oh, I am so sorry, little human."

"Rel is fine."

"Okay Rel. I am called Bear. We are almost there, just twenty more miles."

My eyes bugged out of my head, I collapsed onto the ground.

"We've already gone thirty miles."

"I jest. We are very close. Right over that ridge and down a ways then we are there." He put his hand out and smiled. I grabbed it and pulled myself up. I walked over to the ridge and looked down. There was a castle or palace more like. The turrets spiraled up into the air and thrust through the clouds, I was among the clouds looking down on it. The palace seemed as if it got bored of the color it was every once in a while, so it switched to a new one. At the moment, it seemed to like blue and was changing between the different hues.

"Wow! Just wow. It's magnificent."

"Just a quick climb down, or climb for you—I can fly, and we will be at the gates."

A staircase was growing from the side of the palace and coming to meet the ridge.

"Can't I just use the staircase?"

"What staircase?" He glanced over and saw it. "Holy Guacamole and cheese. What did you do?! That never ever, ever, ever, ever happens. The palace must really like you."

"I have absolutely no idea what to say to that. It's not every day that you get told a building, even a fairy palace, likes you."

"Really? Don't your buildings have feelings?"

"Um, no. My building won't move unless a person moves them, or a powerful windstorm comes through."

"Oh dear, I think it's leaving." I looked around wondering what he was talking about. I saw the bridge receding. I pulled myself over the ridge and hopped down onto the bridge.

"I made it," I gasped. Bear swiveled around to look at me.

"Really, what are you doing down there?"

"I jumped. Why?"

"You didn't get attacked by a dragon?"

"I wouldn't be right here if I had, would I?"

"Well, I guess not. But dragons are really protective of air space and usually attack anything that doesn't belong in the air; they are also really fast."

"Wait really?! I thought you were joking!" The staircase began moving and I fell. I freaked out. "Dragons?! I could have died." I grabbed the railing and pulled myself up, still shaky.

"I suppose so." He flew down to the staircase landing.

"Come on Rel, we are almost there." He walked up the staircase to me and grabbed my wrist and started to pull me.

"I can walk on my own." I pulled my wrist away.

Bear looked a little confused but seemed to accept it. He walked into the palace. I followed not sure what else to do. The staircases were all grand staircases or at least it looked like it.

"Where are we going?"

"To the library, Master Aveil is very smart and sees all."

"Oh," I said, remembering that a library was where this all started. We went down several staircases each encrusted with precious jewels. "Do you ever worry about people stealing the staircases?"

"No, my people are not like yours, they don't steal." Bear pulled me through a door that he must have opened when I was admiring the palace. The room was filled with chestnut wood shelves all lined up in perfectly confusing rows, each curving and twisting to its desires then shifting to compensate for others. Fairies flew around the library pulling books from the shelves and flinging them at each other. Books were hitting shelves then getting pulled into the shelf only to be pulled out once again. Only one fairy looked composed, the wizened fairy sitting at a desk in the middle of the room.

"Bear, how nice to see you again. Who is the little one?" A book flew my way then dropped like a stone in a pond. I glanced over at a girl with flaming red hair and silver wings who gave me an apologetic look.

"Rel, Master Aveil. We are seeking information, but you know that."

"Yea, Jack Jeneiro. You will find him wandering around outside."

"Really?!" I interjected.

"No, he is wandering around 60 miles from here as the crow flies, 100 miles by the road."

"Jeez Louise."

"Who is Louise? Is she your friend? Why are you talking to her? Is she invisible?" Bear looked around searching for what he thought was my invisible friend.

Master Aveil massaged his forehead then spoke.

"Bear, it is an expression of the human world like the one you so like, but I don't think it is one people actually use, you know, 'Holy Guacamole and Cheese.' That was your cue to stop looking around and pay attention to me if you didn't notice."

Bear instantly stopped looking around and became alert. Master Aveil handed Bear a piece of paper.

"I hope you can read maps, Bear, because this is going to be a long journey."

Bear turned white.

"Do you not know how to read a map," I asked.

He shook his head, still looking like he saw a ghost. I grabbed the map and studied it.

The markings were constantly moving and showed every detail as if I was in a helicopter looking down on the place. The names changed too, as if the map realized that people called them different things.

"Doesn't look too complicated," I told Bear even though I was wondering how anyone completely under-stood it.

Bear looked me up and down as if deciding on whether or not to call me crazy.

"I'm serious. Once you get over everything moving it's not that hard. I believe I can figure it out if I try," I said, try-ing to convince myself just as much as I was Bear. Bear just shrugged and made his way over to the door, which I hadn't noticed was carved with intricate patterns. I stopped to feel the carvings, but Bear must have known I would because he grabbed me and pulled me into the hallway.

"Are you sure about this? Maps can usually only be read by scholars, and you don´t look like one. You have no wrinkles," he said, pinching my cheeks. I took his hands off my face.

"Not everyone learns here?"

"Well eventually, but only after you can't fly, which is usually when you are around 930."

"How old do fairies get?" Bear pushed open another door and fairies flooded in chattering about king something or other seeing them.

"As old as they feel like, but most fade away by 4000. We should sneak away before those people realize we opened the gates to get away and did not grant them an audience." He hurried out the door and started running down the stairs which were in the front of the palace, not noticeable at the ridge. I followed when the fairies started swarming like angry bees. Angry screams filled the air. I started sprinting after Bear. We escaped the angry mob and hurried into the trees opposite to the ridge. I plopped to the ground under a tree and pulled the map out of my pocket. I pointed to the landmark close to a blue mark labeled: Jack Jeneiro.

"Where is this?"

"Hampduff Crag?" I nodded even though I was not really sure what he was talking about. "It's that way." He pointed towards some mountains covered in snow. "Is that where Jack is? Wait, is Jack the person that destroyed Jubronica?"

"Um, sure." Bear turned in that direction and walked off. "Are you coming or are you going to gawk at the mountains all day?"

I hurried to catch up. The trees did not last long and soon we were at the base of the mountain. The mountains were magnificent but once we climbed them, or I climbed (Bear flew), we could see Jack descending, a dark splotch on a white background.

I was upset when I saw which way he was going. "Why didn't you turn us around when it was obvious that he was turning around?!"

"Well, I'm sorry that the map only shows the general area of Jack. The blue mark covers several hundred feet."

"Learn to read the map better!"

"I never learned," Bear said.

"I'm trying my best here. If you don't want me to read it, you read it!" Bear quieted at this remark.

"Alright, where's he going now," Bear asked. I looked at the map yet again. I stabbed the map with my finger at another place far from the mountains.

"How did he move so fast?"

"He must have hit a fast patch."

"A fast patch?"

"Oh right, you aren't from here. A fast patch is a piece of land that makes people travel faster than usual."

"He disappeared."

"How did he disappear? That map reaches every place in Elysia… Oh."

"Exactly, he isn't in Elysia anymore, Jack must have gone back to Earth."

"I can't go to Earth," Bear said.

"What do you mean?"

"I don't have my crossing permit yet so I can't cross over portals." I had to follow Jack on my own without any help.

"Where's the portal?"

"I'll bring you there, I can go that far." I thanked Bear and we headed towards the portal. The portal wasn't glowing like the others I had seen, which Bear explained meant this was a portal just between Earth and Elysia so it didn't have a barrier glow from Ramas. The guards of the portal walked up to us.

"Can I see your crossing permit?" Bear answered
for me.

"She's human, humans don't have crossing permits,
the only ones that know about us are the barrier keepers
and she's one of them." The guards looked surprised but
let me through, nonetheless.

I looked around. Trees surrounded me, the many
colors of fall. I pulled the map out to see if it worked on
Earth. To my surprise, the blue mark popped up. A pink
mark popped up as well marked with my name as if being
by a fairy blotted out your mark temporarily. I walked one
way to see which way I had to head to reach Jack; my mark
moved to the left of Jack's, so I straightened out and headed
that way. I eventually hit a road which Jack's mark followed,
so I did too.

The gravel crunched under my feet; with every step my
mark came closer to Jack's. Soon the marks bled into each
other creating purple. I knew Jack was around here somewhere. Leaves lined the edge of the road, all red, yellow,
and orange.

A truck roared and the air filled with exhaust.
The leaves on a bush rustled, and I jerked around.
A jackrabbit bounced out of the bush. I relaxed.

The smell of forests had always had a calming effect
on me. I began to enjoy the scenery taking it all in. The
birds' singing became more noticeable. I saw squirrels
scampering across knobby branches. I reached my hand
up and touched the branches hanging over the road.
Brilliant red leaves flaked from the trees and landed in
my hair. A murder of crows flew overhead filling me with
apprehension once again. I saw a flash of color, a blue jacket,
Jack's jacket. I followed.

The dirt road merged with a main road. I followed
Jack for a while along this road, then he disappeared, and
a purple glow invited me to come to it from across the road.
I waited for the road to be clear which took about three

hours for there to be a gap big enough for me to sprint through without danger of being hit by a car. I ran across the road and dived through the underbrush and through the portal to Elysia. I ran straight into Bear, again.

"I knew you were going to come through this portal again, sadly I was too slow to get here to catch Jack."

"Why are you helping me, Bear? For all you know this could be a wild goose chase."

"I always wanted an adventure, and one ran into me, twice." He chuckled at his own joke. Another fairy, older than Bear, suddenly attacked. Bear whipped out a sword that gleamed in the dying sun and blocked the attack.

"Good job soldier, you should always be at your ready," the fairy said.

He looked at me. "So should you, little butterfly." He pulled another sword out of somewhere and handed it to me. I think fairies have hidden pouches because they always have everything ready no matter what they need. The sword felt heavy and awkward in my hands.

The fairy spoke again. "Teach her, Bear, she will need it." And with that the fairy flew away, leaving me clutching a sword. Thus began my sword lessons.

"Hold the sword up, your enemy could kill you very easily if you let your sword droop." Every spare moment Bear taught me: after breakfast, while we were walking, sometimes even right before I closed my eyes to go to sleep. Eventually Bear deemed me able to hold my own with a sword, at least until help came.

"You are a fast learner. It took me 200 years to get where you are right now."

"How old are you?"

"Only 340, I'm very young. How old are you?" I guessed that Bear was old by human standards but that surprised me.

"Um, this might sound absolutely insane but I'm only 15."

"15?! You are still a baby. Where are your parents, don't they take care of you?"

"I'm actually a teenager by Earth standards. My parents died in a car accident when I was four. I was raised by my grandparents, but a dragon at them up about a year ago." I had looked down while saying this but when I looked up, Bear's face looked so sorrowful I wanted to cry.

"I'm sorry. I shouldn't have asked."

"Oh, it's fine. Look on the bright side. Now I'm here in Elysia, I wouldn't have seen this place for years, I got to see it early." I looked down at the map; we were so close to Jack we were practically on top of him. I glanced up and saw him.

"So touching. Lovely to see you again, Rel."

I tackled him to the ground. He pushed me off, and also bit me, which I don't think was completely on purpose. He pulled himself up and tugged a sword out of nowhere and swung at me. I wrenched my sword out of the sheath and blocked it. This surprised Jack enough to give me time to get up. We parried back and forth for a while then Jack swung hard and fast, pushing me back. I left an opening which I didn't think he would take but he swiped at me leaving a cut deep in my side. Then he got too excited to finish me off and missed the kill strike, I caught him on his way past me in his leg.

Bear was arguing with someone, but I didn't let that distract me too much. "She'll die, I have to help."

"Leave her be, soldier. She must fight her first battle on her own. If you help her then she will never have a first battle." It all faded to background noise.

Another low strike, I struck again this time in the arm. I struck high just like Bear said I would, Jack took the opportunity to hit me in the thigh. My leg crumbled beneath me. It was a wonder that Jack was still standing. I got the advantage of being low to the ground and Jack tripped over me, giving me the ability to whack his back with the sharp of my sword before he got up.

The battle went on for a while eventually depending on who didn't have enough strength to block the other's attack. My vision blurred. I was leaning on my sword. I would not be the first one to pass out from blood loss. Finally, Jack passed out and I followed soon after.

The last thing I heard was: "That girl sure is stubborn. She was losing so much blood but refused to be the first to fall. We could use someone like her. Captain, can we help now?" I never heard the answer.

Somehow, I ended up in a clean bed and my wounds were mostly fixed. Jack ended up in a jail cell at the palace (they fixed him up too). I ended up watching the jail cell through a TV. Jack seemed to be having an extremely violent internal conflict. It was really weird to listen to, (yes, there was a sound system). Mainly: "Dad, please just leave. I want to have a normal life."

"No and no." Weird look at nobody. Disgusted groan. Slapping himself or running into the wall. Me being super confused. One of the nurses, as I came to call them, came in one day during one of these weird exchanges Jack had with himself and decided to check it out.

She came back and told me that Jack had two souls. I made a face. "They aren't both his. One is older but seems linked to the boy, the other is his," was her way of making me understand.

"I want to go talk to him." She helped me to the cell and left me to talk to him. "Who are you?"

"Jack, just like always."

"No really. I know there are two of you." He jolted.

His eyes changed from a hard blue to a soft green. "I'm Jack. The other is my father and deranged. I'm so sorry." Tears ran down his face. He seemed sincere but I didn't know how I could be certain.

I stared across the room at him as I tried to figure it out. I decided to figure it out in my room. I pulled myself to the door.

He said, "Do you need help? I can…"

I looked out the door. Mela was the closest nurse, I wondered where the other nurse had gone.

"Not yours. Mela, can you help me back to my room?" She popped her head around the door frame.

"Of course, of course, of course. I can help, I always want to help."

"Mela, just help me to my room." She put her arm around me and brought me a few corridors over to my room. I plopped myself down onto my bed. Mela started to leave. "Mela, where can I get more information about, um, possession, without having to ask Master Aveil."

"Well, the best place is the library. The library has many books." Her head was bobbing around. I needed to interrupt her before her head came off.

"Mela, just get me the book." Mela hurried away and was back in less time than I thought possible. She handed me the book then rushed off to attend to her other duties. The book was filled with detailed explanations and drawings. It took me a while to finish but when I did, I had a much better understanding of possession.

I got up and started walking around the room and was almost instantly attacked by nurses who must have been wandering outside. Choruses of "you aren't better yet" filled the room. I was getting annoyed, so I yelled at the top of my lungs.

"I'm absolutely fine. Go away." To my surprise, they actually listened! I decided to head back home with Jack in tow. I formulated a plan to get back home and trap Jack. As part of my plan, I asked the fairies to put a guard around Jack so he couldn't cause damage as his father.

They complied and soon we were on our way back. Jack or his dad, depending on the day or time, chattered the whole time as I dragged them along.

"Ugh, will you stop? I can't think of talking with you
so much."

"Have you not been listening to what I've been saying,
it's very interesting," Blue eyes said; Jack's dad wouldn't tell
me his name.

"Why would I listen to your tales of destroying things?
Jack is more interesting, and he has talked about how annoying you are."

"Have you ever dreamed of destroying the world?"

"No, I'm not a psychopath," I said firmly.

"Are you sure?"

"Yes, I'm sure."

"Ha, I made you talk to me."

"What is wrong with you? You sound like you're
younger than me." His eyes turned green. Actual Jack
was back.

"What do you think is wrong with him?"

"I think he has a severe case of immaturity."
He squinted.

"No, it's my turn. You had three hours of control."

"What?"

"Oh sorry," he said. "Did I speak aloud?"

I nodded.

He continued. "Sorry, usually I speak to my father
in my head but I guess it just didn't happen this time."

I quirked my eyebrow.

"You don't control that?"

"No, how could I?"

I shrugged. Then my feet slipped out from under
me, and I slid down a hill. When I reached the bottom,
I realized that I had gone through another portal of realms,
this one only connecting Elysia and Earth.

I landed in a pine tree and instantly started falling
through the branches, scraping my arms and legs. I hit
the ground and pain shot through my shoulder and hip.
Jack landed beside me but on his feet.

"Are you ok?"

"I have absolutely no idea if I'm ok, but I hurt every-where. Whoever created that portal was not very smart." I twisted so I could look at him and found new pain. I looked at Jack's face and found worry and confusion.

"Do you need help? What do you want me to do?" Jack saying this reminded me of the last time he asked if I needed help and I refused him. I tried to pull myself up and almost screamed with the agony of the pain. It wasn't as bad as my fight with Jack, but I felt still pretty bad.

"Yeah, I probably need help. I believe falling through a tree was not the best course of action."

Jack started laughing. Once he had calmed down enough to talk, he looked me up and down, probably as-sessing how best to help me, or maybe he was arguing with his dad. His face was very solemn. I giggled and instantly clutched my stomach.

"What's so funny? Also, falling through a tree should not do that much damage."

"Nothing. And who says."

Jack looked a little annoyed.

"I'm kidding, I think it's mostly old wounds that were clawed open. The one on my side sure was." Jack contemplated this.

"So, what you're saying is to be careful." I nodded feeling like an invalid.

He grabbed my shoulders and pulled me into a sitting position. He stopped to give me a moment to get over the pain then grabbed me under the arms and tugged me to standing. A scream escaped my lips.

"Sorry, do you know where we are?" He readjusted so he was holding me up, but I could look around. My vision blurred and I knew I was going to be unconscious soon and since I wasn't fighting anyone and blue eyes couldn't hurt me that didn't bother me one bit.

"We're about two miles from Austin." Then I passed out.

The amazing thing about sleep is if you go into a deep enough sleep, pain is nonexistent. I woke up in a farmhouse, surrounded by boys. I shrieked.

"Shrilly one, isn't she," the tallest one said laughing.

"Lay off, will you? Food's ready. How about you, dear, do you feel like food? You were beat up pretty bad. You're lucky your brother was there or maybe some animal would have finished you off." A woman who must have been the boys' mother was standing above me, her blonde hair falling into her grey eyes.

I tried to sit up, which is not easy with five heavy quilts piled on top of you. She laughed, not a mean laugh but a beautiful, full laugh. She put pillows under me and went to get something.

I looked around. The house was whitewashed, and pictures hung absolutely everywhere. There were pictures of little boys on every wall, but my eyes lingered on one of a little boy sitting on his dad's shoulders. The boy who laughed at me looked embarrassed but didn't do anything else. I searched the room for Jack.

He sat at the table shoveling food in his mouth like he would never see it again. I tried to get his attention; eventually he glanced over and I signaled him with my head to come over. He scooted his chair out and came over.

"Will you take these off me? They are crushing the air out of me. Also, who are these people?" I whispered. Jack pulled one quilt after another off me and gradually the pressure came off my ribcage which was probably broken in some places.

"The lady is Rae Thomas. The boys are Lawrence, Luke, Liam, and Leo." Jack pointed to each in turn. Rae came over to me.

"Apparently your brother doesn't know where you live, where do we need to bring you? Or can your parents bring you?"

"We live in Sparks. Our parents are away right now."

I felt bad even semi-lying to her, but she could get us in serious trouble.

"What are you doing so far from home?"

"We came this way with some friends but then they left us behind so I guess you can say they aren't really friends," Jack lied.

"Oh, well, let's all get in the car…". Jack's eyes turned blue. "Alright, let's go," Blue eyes said.

Luke (or at least I think it was Luke: all the boys look the same—tall, blonde hair, blue eyes) noticed that nobody was helping me so turned and pulled the rest of the quilts off me.

"I think you can walk now without all those quilts on you." He winked and walked away.

I swung my feet over the edge of what I would call a bed though it could also be classified as a window seat. I found I was not wearing the black shirt and khakis I had been wearing when I crashed. Instead. I was wearing a flowery dress that came down to mid-calf, an annoying length. I saw my shoes by the door and pulled them on.

I followed everyone out the door and to the driveway. A blue suburban was parked there. We all piled in, Rae driving and the rest of us in the back. The car ride was pretty enjoyable, filled with singing and a few wrong turns. The only annoying part was blue eyes' gruff remarks every once in awhile. Soon we turned into Sparks.

"Just drop us off here, we can get to our house from here. Thank you so much," I said, stopping us close to the portal of realms. I got out and pulled blue eyes along with me. Rae and her family left without a word, but I hoped to stay in contact with them. I shoved blue eyes through the hedge and prepared my mind for my plan.

I stepped through the hedge and led blue eyes through the clearing towards Ramas. I put him halfway through the portal. I started chanting the barrier enchantment but left it barely unfinished then started another enchantment that

I found in the book I had read. As promised, the souls separated leaving Jack with his, I pulled Jack back through the barrier and finished the barrier enchantment.

I looked at Jack. He was smiling for the first time ever. I smiled back.

"We should probably get home. I want to see if I can find my family." He glanced back as he walked ahead of me. "If I find them you should come with me and be part of a family again."

I readily agreed. Living alone was well, lonely, and having a family again would be wonderful.

# THE SNOBANES



Rook was doing his homework, frustrated that he couldn't understand it. Lilila was reading a book. Jett was doing the dishes. Sara was in her room playing. Cherie was wiping at the windows furiously. Carla and Tim were dancing and singing random songs. Opa was reading the newspaper. Oma was dusting.

DING-DONG. "A letter for the Snowbanes," a voice said.

Sara rushed to the door, starting to unlock the seven locks. Then Jett stopped her, reached through the window and grabbed the letter from gloved hands. Jett sets the paper down and walks over and looks at the letter.

"What's it say, Jett," Opa questioned.

"It's asking for us to come for screenings," Jett answered.

Sara tugged on Jett's shirt. "What's a screening," she asked. Jett started to talk but Opa interrupted.

"We aren't going so you don't have to worry," Opa said, picking up Sara.

Rook looked up. "Can somebody help me with this?" he shouted from the other room. Lilila laughed.

"What question are you on?," Lilila asked as she sat down next to Rook.

He looked down at the paper that had smudges all over it. Lilila laughed again." I think you need another eraser," she laughed, "and maybe a new piece of paper."

Soon they were done, and Rook went out to herd the cows. Puffball followed him out.

The next day there was a sharp knocking on the door. "Open up. This is the Future Apprehension Team," a F.A.T. man called from outside. There was a buzzing and the door fell open. Rook stopped playing his tenor sax. Sara screamed and ran past the agent, her blonde hair whipping behind her. There was a scraping sound on vinyl and grunting sounds from the front room. There was a great scuffle then silence. Rook ran into the front room with the saxophone banging against his knees. He looked everywhere but everyone was gone.

Rook looked in Puffball's cage. No Sara. He looked in the kitchen. No Oma. He looked in the living room, the conservatory, the bathrooms. No Jett, Carla, Opa, Lilila, Cherie, or Tim. But he did find Puffball and Willow locked in a closet. He looked outside. No family.

Rook shuffled to his room and plopped down on his bed. Where was the rest of his family? He thought for a while. Then he went to the kitchen and grabbed a piece of pie. Rook scurried back to his room and looked in a drawer. No notebook, no pen either. He looked in another drawer, and a green notebook was in it. He flung the notebook onto his bed and started rummaging through other drawers. Rook noticed whipped cream on his sweater and put the pie on his dresser. Then out of the corner of his eye Rook saw a bright pink pencil under his nightstand. He grabbed it, snatched his notebook, and threw them onto the table. Then he rushed back to grab the pie. When he was finally sitting down, he noticed his tenor sax was still around his neck and he ran back to his room to put it back on its hook.

When he sat down knowing he didn't have anything else to do, he started writing ideas. Did they … no they wouldn't. What if they … nope, that's outrageous. Then he remembered the letter they had received the day before. He went and retrieved it from the trash and read it. It said:

*"Snowbanes-*

*"Come to Helena, Montana for screening.*
*If you don't you will regret it.*

*~Future Apprehension Team"*

They must be at the gel cells, Rook realized. He grabbed his jacket and rushed to the door. He put in the codes for four of the seven locks and skipped out the door with the key. He brought out his ipod and looked up "Gel cells." It didn't work, so he hacked the server so he could get there—Something he had learned from Lilila. The website said, "Is under the museum at 1097 East 1500 North, Terreton, Idaho."

"That museum, it's one I've been to so many times. I can't believe it," Rook shouted. And he headed out.

Then, Mr. Xander looked over from next door. Rook looked down and kept going. When he got there, he opened the door and saw a trap door under a display. He moved it and lifted up, the trapdoor. There was a set of bronze-colored stairs. He tramped down them trying not to clang with his cowboy boots.

He reached the bottom and saw a container with lime green gel in it with the faint outline of a human in it. Rook ran over and pounded on the glass. A Humanoid glanced over at the gel cell, but Rook had already hid behind it. Rook looked up at a sign he had seen from the corner of his eye; it said: "Open here." There was a button beneath it; he pushed the button then backed away.

A door opened on the gel cell and a limp body fell onto the ground. Rook turned it over and his eyes widened, it was Olivia Sadry from school! She started coughing violently. Rook looked around the gel cell to make sure there were no humanoids.  He turned back to Olivia. She had sat up and was looking confused.

Then she saw him and smiled. "I'm so glad it's you. Those stupid humanoids were going to brainwash me today," she whispered. "We have to get out of here."

"I know we do but I have to find the rest of my family," Rook replied. They looked in all the gel cells and eventually they found someone. It was also someone Rook recognized… it was Sara!

Rook's eyes wandered around and then he freaked out. There was no open button on this cell. 'Think, think, think,

think," Rook mumbled. Then his eyes lit up. "Climb on my shoulders and see if there is a button on top anywhere," he pleaded.

"Yes! There is one. I'm going to push it!" Olivia shouted.

"Not so loud, Olivia," Rook whispered up to her.

Olivia's hand came down, then they toppled over. Green gel squirted everywhere, and Sara flailed through the air. She smacked into Rook knocking the wind out of him and knocking him down. Sara jumped up and looked around. She seemed content.

They tiptoed over to an elevator under the stairs, and it opened. They froze, but Olivia giggled. Rook looked at her quizzingly, so she explained in a whisper, "The elevator has sensors that open the doors based on movement."

They stepped inside the elevator and looked for the buttons to make it move. They found them on the ceiling and Olivia gave Rook a look of distress, noting that the ceiling was twice their size.

"You can climb on my shoulders and push it," Rook said with a laugh.

They were a tiny bit too short, so Sara clambered up on top of Olivia and slapped the button. They got to the first floor in no time. When they came out, they came face to face with the jack rabbit round-up display. They sneaked past it, but then a robotic voice shouted

"YOU ARE TRESPASSING ON PRIVATE PROPERTY."

They bolted past it and pushed through the door.

Olivia grabbed Sara and put her on her shoulders.

"YOU ARE TRESPASSING ON PRIVATE PROPERTY," the voice said again.

Olivia and Rook kept running. Rook tripped and fell to the rocky road. He jumped up and kept sprinting.

"I can't believe that I did that," Rook muttered.

"Rook, Rook!" a person said from behind. He looked back. It was Lilila!

"Rook, where should we go," Olivia shouted back at him, worry spreading across her face. Rook glanced back. The F.A.T. men and humanoids were less than five feet away. He looked forward again and he saw his street. It was four blocks away.

"Turn on Chastain Road," Rook almost screamed. Olivia was advancing on Chastain Road, then she turned onto it and hid behind some trees. Rook put on full speed, and he gained at least seven feet on their pursuers. He was almost there. He skidded to a stop.

He turned onto his street. Olivia came out from where she was hiding and ran with him. They jogged past several houses before getting to his house. When they got there, the door flung open.

"Stay here, there may be F.A.T. men inside," Rook whispered frantically.

He crept inside; there was a shadow under the table so he hesitated. When he moved again, something grabbed his leg and he yelped. He looked down. It was Carla! Then Tim came out from under the table and gestured outside. "Are you going to let that girl, Sara, and Lilila inside," Tim chuckled.

Rook opened the door and they all filed inside. Tim closed the door behind them and put a huge padlock on the door.

"Rook, next time, don't freak out when the" ...the padlock buzzed…" family disappears. We can take care of ourselves." No sooner had Lilila finished this sentence when the padlock flew off the door. Everyone ducked and the padlock banged into the stove. The door was flung open wide and there were Opa, Oma, and Cherie.

Olivia was on the verge of screaming, you could tell by looking at her face.

Everyone laughed. Olivia calmed down.

"We didn't think you would lock us out," Cherie laughed.

"How did you get out?" Tim asked.

"Just some high-tech engineering. Well, actually, we used a drill. Those humanoid things are so dumb," Cherie told him.

"You guys, I have something to tell you, mostly about the president's plans, but it's a long story," Olivia admitted.

"Go ahead dear, tell us everything we have lots of time," Oma said gently.

"Well, first of all, Rook, I should probably tell your family who I am," Olivia said. Rook nodded. "I am Olivia Sadry. I am in a couple of Rook's classes at school," Olivia explained. "Did I miss something?"

"I don't think so," Rook said.

"All right, so I was walking around the weather observatory, when I noticed the trap door was open at the museum. I walked down the stairs because I was curious. I heard a voice when I got down there, it was the president! 'What do you suppose we do, Doctor?'" he asked.

"We should get all the people in your country and bring them here, brainwash them and make them into your army so then when we go to invade Germany, they don't know what hit them and the people we lose won't matter. And then we can invade other places too like…"

*Sniff sniff sniff,*

"There is someone here. Humanoids attack!"

Suddenly the air was filled with robot voices saying something and they all grabbed me and brought me to the Doctor and the president, who said, "Young lady, has no one ever told you that it is rude to eavesdrop?"

"Well, nobody told me not to eavesdrop on people with evil plans. In fact, they encouraged it," I said.

"Then the doctor screamed, 'Take her away.'"

"Sorry I'm interrupting myself, but he looked kinda like Albert Einstein and sounded like the mad scientist from the movie, *Igor.* It was super weird."

Everyone laughed except Sara who said, "What does Albert Einstein look like?"

"He had white crazy hair that stuck out in all directions," Olivia answered. "Well, anyway, they put me in the gel cell and I was in suspended animation, I think. Then about two days ago, they opened the cell and said they would take me to a lab in another two days, and I've been there ever since."

"Okay, I just realized that was not a very long story," Olivia finished.

*We knew our adventure wasn't over but everyone was hungry so we ordered pizza and wondered what our next steps should be.*

*TO BE CONTINUED*

# MCKELLE
## SNEDAKER

# SARIELLE, THE MEDIEVAL PRINCESS

"On that night, the day after my tenth birthday, they never came back."

"What happened to them?"

"I don't know, and if I don't find out soon, I'll never be able to go home again."

"Tell me what you remember about that day. I want to help you."

"I remember I was excited about the present they had given me. It was my necklace, this one, the one I am wearing, the one I've worn every day since then." The girl said, holding up her turquoise necklace.

"It is a beautiful necklace. It makes you even more beautiful than you already are."

"Thank you," she said with a blush.

"Sorry to distract, continue."

"Anyways, I was admiring my necklace when my parents, the King and Queen of Avinne, came in to tell me they were going for a ride on the boat. They asked me if I wanted to go with them. I told them I didn't want to, I wanted to stay and keep admiring my present. "Then they left, and I never saw them ever again."

"I'm so sorry. Did anyone go with them, or even see what happened?"

"No, no one was with them. All anyone knew was that they found the boat they were using shipwrecked somewhere in the kingdom. The boat was almost completely destroyed. Everyone knew they didn't survive when they saw it—no one could have survived. Everyone knew they could not have disembarked fast enough, that they had been defeated. I just wish I could have known then what had happened to them, I want to know now. I wish I could have saved them."

"You couldn't have. From what you've heard, nobody could have."

"I know. I just wish they were still here, I wish they were still alive."

"I'm sure."

"Of course, I miss them and would have liked some parent help in my life, but that's not the only reason I wish they were still here. If they had been here, then I wouldn't have had to be locked in my room all my life. I would have been able to enjoy my childhood, I would have been able to know more people than just Azura and Sirius."

"Wait, you have been stuck in your room for six years and now you're finally outside again?"

"Yes."

"Why would the guards be so strict?"

"Since they didn't know how my parents had died exactly, they were afraid my people would turn against me. As you have seen, I am very trusting, and they were afraid I would trust someone who would want to hurt me."

"Tell me how you got here again. How you, Azura, and Sirius met Issac, Briana, and me."

"Okay, well, I was having the same, normal, routine day I have every day, until lately, as you know. Then, a guard banged the door open, which no one had ever done before. They were forbidden of it, and he yelled 'A man's coming, coming straight for you. He's using magic to kill anyone in his way, Princess, you're not safe here!' Then he grabbed my hand and took me, Azura, and Sirius to the throne room that I had not been in in six whole years. There were many guards, all armed, and in the middle of them was the captain of the guard. I don't remember his name. He told me he had to use magic to get me somewhere safe. I was alarmed by this, because we never used magic, not unless it was absolutely necessary, so I knew this was important. He opened a portal through time and space. Then he said, 'The only way for you to get home again is to delve and find the truth about what happened to your parents. We will then be summoned to come and get you if it is safe.' By then we could hear

screaming in the hall, the deafening scream of death,
as Azura, Sirius, and I jumped into the portal. The closest
thing I remember after that is waking up on a beach with
you standing over me. You were concerned and wearing
those weird clothes. What is it called again?"

"A swimsuit."

"Yes, a swimsuit, and Bianca and Issac were with you,
and both of them were wearing one as well. They were
making sure Azura and Sirius were okay, and you were
checking me."

"Yes."

"Then you took us somewhere, your house you called it?"

"Yes, our home."

"You gave us food and water and kept us warm. Then
you asked about our story, how we had gotten there on the
beach, knocked out in the middle of the day. I told you what
happened, but you didn't believe me."

"No, I didn't, I thought you were delusional, that the sun
had fried your brain," Benedict said with a laugh.

"I'm sure I would have thought the same if I were in
your shoes."

"Yeah."

"Then, against what I have been taught, I showed
you magic."

"Hmm, I remember. You showed us your necklace
that started glowing and you told me exactly what I was
thinking, including everyone else." He said as his face
turned bright red.

"You were thinking how beautiful I was. I won't go into
what the others were because I already told you."

"Yep."

"Then somehow we convinced you three to help us. We
said that to know what we needed to know, we needed a pool
of clear water at midnight. It would show us what we needed.
In our case, how my parents were killed."

"I'm still so sorry about that."

"You've already said that so many times, it's not your fault." She said with a smile. "Then you told us about Blue Lake and how you thought it would work. You said you all hiked there a lot and that the water was always so clear. By the way, I don't think you still believed us at that point."

"You're probably right."

"Then you and Issac told your parents you were going to Blue Lake and were going to camp with some new friends. They said yes, it was OK. Then you drove us all to the, what's it called? Trailhead?"

"Yep, the Trailhead for Blue Lake."

"We walked down here, into this beautiful copse, and have been here now two nights because the moon has been covered by the clouds. Sirius and Bianca, who are both ten, right?"

"Yes, Bianca is ten."

"Anyways, they have become the best of friends, so have Azura and Issac. And we've talked and talked and have become close now too, and I finally think you all believe us about living in the eleventh century."

"Yes, to be honest, I do finally and totally believe you."

"Thank you," she said with a smile. "I do think this will be our last night here though. It looks like the moon is coming up nicely. Soon I should be back in Avinne, being an actual princess and not hiding in my room from who knows who or what."

"Hey, Sarielle, may I ask you a question?" Benedict said, his cheeks warming because he was a little embarrassed.

"Why couldn't you? What do you need?" She asked.

"W-well," he said nervously, "before the others come back from gathering firewood, would you care to dance with me? I-in the firelight? I'm not a good dancer and I know you know how to dance very well. Would you teach me?"

"I would, but there's no music."

"So?" Benedict asked as he stood up and held out his hand to the Princess of Avinne, gaining confidence.

She looked at the hand for a moment, then took and started teaching him how to dance. They were slow at first but got faster and better the longer they danced.

Eventually, they slowed to a stop, looking into each other's eyes. Their faces grew closer and closer. Sarielle closed her eyes and was about to share a passionate kiss when they heard the bushes behind them start to rustle.

They looked toward the bushes and the space between the two grew. The rustling branches were from the others coming back from searching for firewood and berries. "Um. What are you doing?" Issac, Benedict's best friend asked.

"Nothing." They answered at the same time, each taking another step from the other.

Azura and Bianca couldn't help it; they couldn't stop giggling. When Bianca, Benedict's younger sister, had a little more control of herself she said, "Were you just about to kiss?," and started laughing all over again.

"Whatever. Think what you wish," Sarielle said as she started preparing their meager meal of granola bars and fish.

◉◉◉

That night the moon was just what they needed—it was beautiful and bright, and the water in the lake was smooth and clear. It was a perfect night to know what they needed to know.

They walked then swam to the island in the middle of Blue Lake. When they were all on it, they made a half-circle around Sarielle, who was kneeling down near the water.

"This is perfect," she said, "I'll finally know what happened to my parents, and I'll be able to go back home again. And I'll be free!"

Everyone watched as the reflection of the moon right in front of them started to shimmer. It started to show a beautiful, sunny day with a handsome couple in a small boat, staring at each other with obvious love.

Sarielle gasped, "It's them" she cried, "it's really them! They're just like I remember!"

Then, out of nowhere, dark, billowing clouds came into the picture.

"What's happening?!" asked Bianca with alarm.

No one responded, they were too busy staring at the moving picture in the water.

The couple looked around them. They were confused. Then, out of the dark clouds came a man, an evil man. He was wearing dark clothes with a long, black cape. He wasn't riding anything, he was floating. He was using magic.

Azura could tell something was coming, something terrible and awful, so she grabbed Sirius and Bianca and shielded their faces. They didn't resist; they knew the picture would be one they could never get out of their heads again if they saw.

Eventually, everyone but Sarielle had turned their heads away from the awful picture of horror and death. Everyone was quiet when it was over, Sarielle most of all. She had tears streaming down her face. She wished it could have been her and not them.

"I'll take Sirius and Bianca back to camp." Azura said and she went and gave Sarielle a big hug, "It's okay, you're okay, we're safe."

"I'll go with you," Issac said, not wanting to stay and have Sarielle tell her about the horrible picture, wanting that it should be Benedict who helped Sarielle.

The four left Benedict and Sarielle the way they were and swam back to camp.

Benedict still stood, not sure what to do, but knowing he shouldn't leave Sarielle alone. "Are you okay?" he asked, already knowing she wasn't.

The only response was silence.

He sat down next to her and grabbed her hand, tracing the lines on her palm.

"I want to help, will it help if you talk it out? I didn't see, I couldn't."

"It was awful," she said in a soft voice, "It was him, he did it," she said as she started to sob and Benedict took her into his arms.

"It's okay, you're safe," Benedict said, trying not to push her limits on talking.

"It was him. It was the magician."

"What magician?"

"Our magician, my family's magician. He killed them. It was him. That ominous villain. And now he's after me."

"What? He's after you?" Benedict asked as held her at arm's length, "He's after you? He wants to kill you?"

"Yes, he told them I was next. That's who was after me in the castle. He's the one why I'm here."

"He's not going to hurt you, I won't let him."

"You can't stop him. He's the most powerful magician. He's indefatigable. In Avinne we never use magic unless it is absolutely necessary, and we never use black magic. We are never allowed to hurt anyone with our magic. But Ismzal, our magician," she said bitterly, "well, he uses black magic. He uses it for his gain only, even if that means using it to kill."

"But why, why would he want to hurt you and your family?"

"Because of the prophecy," she said, as if that inspired thought explained everything.

"The prophecy?"

"When I was a baby, my parents were invited to a royal wedding. It was my mothers' cousin who was getting married. She hadn't met me yet, so she just adored me, as momma said. Anyways, their magician came over and held me, too; he said I was special, unique. He told my parents that I would not live forever in my world but in another. He said that this other world was where I ultimately belonged. That I would meet a boy and be changed forever, that I would change the course on my kingdom forever with his help. My mother told me that our magician was angry at this news, and that I was supposed to stay and be the ruler of Avinne.

"Then, when I was seven, I believe, I hit my head extremely hard. Everyone thought I wouldn't survive, but it was a miracle and I lived, as you see me now. I was unconscious for a few days, and during that time I had dreams, such glorious dreams. When I finally woke up I told my parents about them and they kept saying over and over again, 'the prophecy, it's the prophecy.'"

"What were the dreams?"

"I remember they were dreams of a faraway place with a gigantic lake, and there was a full, rushing river coming out of it. I remember there were many people, but the being I remember the most was a boy. He wore strange clothing, in fact, he was wearing something like that!" Sarielle said excitedly as she pointed to the clothes Benedict was wearing.

"The end, well, I'm embarrassed to say."

"What? What is it? You don't have to be embarrassed."

"No, I'll skip it, it's embarrassing."

"Come on, what is it?"

"Fine, I'll tell you. At the end of my dream, there was lots of white and I was wearing my mother's royal crown."

"What happened?" Benedict asked, dying to know now.

"Well, the boy and I," she said, talking slowly as she gathered her thoughts, "everything was white, a-and the boy and I kissed, and started laughing."

"Whoa, I wasn't expecting that!" He said, startled, then, "Wait, you said I was the boy, right?"

"I don't know for sure, but you do look like how I remember him."

"Okay, well then, why don't we have that kiss. What do you say?" Benedict said as his face neared hers.

"I say," Sarielle continued, "I say, yes."

Just as their lips were about to touch, there was another interruption.

"Benedict, Sarielle, watch out!!" Someone from their party yelled.

They both looked up and saw the same dark, billowing clouds as they had watched in the moving-water picture. A man came out of the clouds. Ismzal, Sarielle's family magician. "It's him! It's him!" Sarielle yelled at Benedict over the noise and pointed at the descending figure.

"I won't let him hurt you," Benedict yelled back, knowing she was scared.

"You can't stop him. If you try he will only kill you too. Please don't try."

"I can't just sit here and watch as he murders you! I love you Sarielle, and I can't watch that or even let it happen!"

"Y-you love me?"

"Of course, I do, who wouldn't? You're the most beautiful, most kind, most forgiving, and generous person out there. I love you Sarielle, princess, and heir to the throne of Avinne, I love you with all my heart."

"I love you too, but I have to do this on my own. I can't let you get hurt because of me."

Benedict was about to protest when the evil magician said with a very loud voice as he touched down on the island, "Why, hello there, little princess." His voice sounded empty. "Do you remember me?"

"Of course I do, my parents trusted you. Why did you kill them, why are you trying to kill me?"

"Well, that's simple. I want your throne, I want that prophecy of you to disappear into thin air, I want you to be my servant like I had once been to you."

Sarielle glanced back at Benedict, hoping to gain some strength. "You will never have my crown and I will never be your servant."

"Well, then that leaves only one option, doesn't it? I will just kill you instead and inherit the throne because I was the royal magician."

"You will never hurt her! If you want to, you'll have to go through me!" Benedict said, stepping in front of Sarielle.

"You'll have to go through us as well!"

The three turned around to see Sarielle and Benedict's friends coming up behind them. Sarielle couldn't take it any longer, "No, just take me, and leave them alone! Please, don't hurt them."

Ismzal got this creepy, snake-like smile on his face, "Oh I see, you want them to be safe, but you don't care about yourself. You know what, I've changed my mind, I won't kill you."

"You won't?!" everyone asked at the same time.

"I won't, I'll just make you suffer by taking your friends and making them my slaves and leave you helpless and alone."

"NO!" Sarielle shouted as Ismzal used his dark magic to pick up her friends and take them to his evil hideout.

The last thing Sarielle remembered as everything around her went black, was the evil laugh of Ismzal.

◉◉◉

The next thing Sarielle remembered was a man picking her up. She was dripping wet from being left in the water so long, and he took her away.

◉◉◉

When she finally fully woke up, she was in a white room wearing strange clothes. It was dark outside, but bright in the room. She could hear a constant beep and a bag of what looked like water was attached to her arm.

In a second, everything came back to her. How her parents had died, Benedict saying he loved her, and Ismzal kidnapping her friends. She didn't think she could do it, she didn't think she could go on and save her friends. She was at her breaking point, her breach, so she sat in that strange room wearing those strange clothes, and cried. She cried her heart and soul out, eventually crying herself to sleep.

The next morning Sarielle woke up to a nicely dressed young woman checking the beeping machine and the water tube attached to her arm,

"Who are you? Where am I?" Sarielle asked.

"You are at the Cascade Medical Center," the woman said, "and I am nurse Ada Rush. You can just call me Ada."

"Why am I here?"

"You were up at Blue Lake, unconscious in the water. A Fish and Game warden saw you and brought you here. You should be released today, we just wanted to make sure you were alright. Why don't you get some sleep?"

"Okay," Sarielle said as she pretended to doze off.

Once the nurse was gone, Sarielle got up and put on her regular clothes that were hanging over a chair. At some time while the nurse had been talking, Sarielle realized that she had to save her friends, that she needed them.

She left the building while no one was looking and found her way around the small town of Cascade, Idaho. She eventually found the road that led up to Blue Lake and she started walking. She found the trailhead and from there the lake itself.

She looked around their campsite that had been taken down by the warden and found nothing. Then she swam out to the island where that awful memory had played itself out. That was where she found what she was looking for, a piece of Ismzal's cape.

All she needed now was to control her magic to take the piece, and her, to where the rest of the cape was. That would be where Ismzal and her friends would be too.

It took a while for her to cast the spell with her necklace, as she had not done such a complicated spell before. She finally did it, however, when she had summoned up enough determination to do so.

"Here we go," Sarielle said as the little piece of cloth acted as a magnet, attracted to the rest of itself.

She followed the direction the cloth pulled her till she reached the edge of Cascade Lake. She was confused about where it was taking her, but she knew it was right. She asked a kind man if he could drive her on his boat to the other side of the lake, maybe. He said yes and they set off.

"Turn right," Sarielle said to the kind man, "please."

They eventually ended up at Sugarloaf Island, and the man dropped her off there. She climbed out and continued following the pull of the tattered piece of cloth until she found a hidden cave leading down.

It was a dark and prodigious cave with cobwebs everywhere. She wished she could turn around, run out, and never return, but she knew she couldn't. She had to save her friends, no matter the consequences.

"No, don't hurt him, please, don't hurt him!" she heard, there was an obvious alarm and trepidation in the voice.

"Bianca!" Sarielle said louder than she meant.

"Oh, I'll hurt him, I'll make her highness suffer. I'll kill him for my own benefit," the formidable Ismzal said with an evil laugh.

Sarielle knew then what was about to happen. Benedict! He's going to kill Benedict! She was now running impetuously down the steep, dark stairs.

When she got to the end of the steps, she saw a horrifying scene. Bianca and Azura were sobbing and holding each other in an awkward position, as they were tied up. Issac and Sirius were standing up next to them, also tied up to a large pole, trying to be brave.

Last but certainly not least, Benedict was tied up, no emotion of his solemn face, to a pole high above the ground, dangling over the evil magician. Ismzal had his hands facing Benedict, getting ready for the kill no doubt.

That's when Sarielle jumped out of hiding, "Stop! You don't want him, you want me!"

"Oh, look who's back to save the day," Ismzal drawled.

Then, extremely fast, he pointed his hands at Sarielle and used his dark magic to throw a very powerful fireball at her.

"Watch out!" someone yelled.

"Benedict? Is that you?" Sarielle said, paying attention to the voice and not the certain death that was coming straight for her.

"Watch out!" Just as the fire was about to hit her someone came out of nowhere and knocked her down and out of the way.

When Sarielle got a grip of what just happened she realized who had just saved her, "Benedict? But how, you were just stuck up there?"

"You're not the only one who can perform a version of magic." He smiled at her. "It's called a pocketknife." Benedict said, holding out the knife for her to see.

"Aw, look, he saved you, isn't that sweet?" Ismzal said with a false sense of kindness. "Now you will die together!" He shouted as he sent another, powerful ball of flaming fire towards the two on the floor.

Sarielle got up fast and sent her own spell towards Ismzal, out of the way of his. Then the ball of fire hit her, and she fell, dead on the floor. In his success Sarielle's spell hit Ismzal, it was a dissolving spell, and he disappeared. He disappeared for good, never to hurt anyone ever again.

"Sarielle!!" Benedict yelled as he ran to her lifeless body, "No, no, no, no, no!" He held her to his chest and rocked her back and forth, crying into her hair, "No, no, no, no." He cried.

By this time everyone was surrounding them, crying. Issac was hugging Azura as she cried, and Bianca and Sirius were holding hands and sitting next to Benedict and the lifeless Sarielle.

After a minute or two, Sarielle's necklace started glowing. It was dim at first and became slowly brighter by degrees.

"Look, her necklace! It is glowing again!" Bianca yelled excitedly as she pointed at the necklace.

Benedict whipped his head up to see this was true and immediately put his head to her heart, "She has a pulse!" he shouted, "She's alive! Sarielle, can you hear me? Can you hear my voice?"

"Give her a minute," Azura said excitedly.

"Benedict?" said a small voice.

"Sarielle? Sarielle, I'm right here! Can you hear me?"

"Benedict, yes, I can hear you." It took a few moments for Sarielle to regain her composure and her smile.

"You make the ambiance in here more cheerful. It was sad and depressing before," Bianca said to Sarielle as they had a big hug.

"That's a big word," Sarielle smiled.

Everyone was shouting for joy now. Their beloved friend was alive and happy, but Azura cut the celebration short, "Let's give them a minute, shall we? Bianca, Sirius, follow Issac and me out, we'll let these two have some privacy."

"Thank you," Benedict said, grateful that Azura could tell he wanted alone time with his medieval princess.

"What happened?" Sarielle asked when they were alone.

"Let's just say Ismzal is gone for good, and you are alive, so life is good."

"No," Sarielle said, "God is good."

"Your right, God is good. In fact, he is more than good, he is the best." Benedict said with a smile, knowing his Sarielle was back.

The two were about to kiss when the others burst in, "The captain of the guard is here, he's taking us home!" Sirius yelled.

◉◉◉

"Well, I guess this is goodbye." Sarielle said before she jumped into the portal. "I'll miss you. Don't forget about me."

"How could I?" Benedict asked. "You are the best thing that ever happened to me."

"I'll miss you!" Sarielle called as the portal closed around her.

"I'll miss you more," Benedict whispered to what was now nothing but used to be the most beautiful girl to ever live on planet Earth.

◉◉◉

They had been back in Avinne for a few weeks now. Sarielle had more of a normal life as a princess, balls every night and in the throne room all day, instead of being locked in her room as she had been before. She had once thought that was all she needed to be happy, but now she knew the truth. What she really needed to be happy was friends she could lean on, especially a handsome boy she loved more than anything.

"Sarielle, you're needed in the… " Azura cut off what she was saying as she walked into the room. "You're thinking of him again, aren't you." It was a statement, not a question.

"No, I'm not," Sarielle said defensively as she turned away from the window. "I-I'm just thinking about…," Sarielle said as she tried to think of something she could be thinking about besides what she really had been thinking about. Giving up, she finally said, "Yes, I was thinking about Benedict again."

"You know what I think?" Azura asked as she walked over to hug her friend, "I think this is what the prophecy meant. You belong in the twenty-first century with Benedict, you don't belong here. I think you should go back. I think you should find him."

"What? But I can't, I have a kingdom to run."

"I'll watch over it for you. You need him, I've seen that ever since we got back."

"Fine, but you'll not just watch over it, you'll be its ruler unless you want to come with me."

"No, I belong in this era. Wait a minute, did you just say what I think you just said?"

"Yes, if you want to be, you can be the crowned ruler of Avinne."

"Really?"

"You have always loved the kingdom more than I have. You'd be a great ruler."

◉◉◉

Azura became the crowned ruler of the kingdom Avinne the next week. It was a beautiful coronation, and Sarielle wished she could be there for the celebration afterward, but she couldn't. She was going to see her true love in his world of the twenty-first century.

Once Azura was officially crowned princess, she and Sarielle said their goodbyes, "I'll miss you so much!"

"I'll miss you more!"

Sirius went up to them and asked, "Sarielle, can I go with you? I want to be with Bianca, and what did they call it? Technology? Please?"

"Sirius, aren't you going to stay here with me?" Azura asked, heartbroken, that her brother wanted someone besides her.

"Please?"

"It'll be okay, I make sure he is good and okay. I won't let anything happen to him," Sarielle said, suddenly wanting someone from her own world with her.

"Okay, I love you, little brother," Azura said as she squeezed him with a hug.

"I love you too, and I'll miss you more!" Sirius called as he and Sarielle grabbed hands and passed through the portal.

◉◉◉

As Sirius and Sarielle walked up to a house they hoped they would get to know very well, Benedict and Bianca's house, someone yelled excitedly, "Benedict, come quick! It's Sirius and Sarielle!" It was Bianca's voice as she came running up and gave Sirius an overwhelming hug.

"What did you say, Bianca?" Benedict asked as he came outside, "Sarielle? Sirius? Sarielle! Sirius!" Benedict shouted as he saw them and he and Sarielle ran into each other's arms.

"What are you doing here? I thought you were back in Avinne. And would be there forever."

"I was in a quandary. I couldn't live like that anymore, even though it was more familiar than here. I gave up the kingdom, and Azura is ruling it, because that's what she wanted. Then I came here to stay, and Sirius came too."

"I've missed you so much! You're finally back!"

"I was aimless those few weeks. Now I have a reason to keep going again. You."

◉◉◉

Four years later, when Sarielle was twenty, Sarielle and Benedict had the best day of their lives. They were married, surrounded by family and friends, including Azura, in the most beautiful place, Blue Lake.

"You may kiss the bride," the priest said, as he finished the special ceremony.

"Are you ready to finally kiss, without being interrupted this time?" Benedict whispered into his bride's ear.

"Ready as I'll ever be," Sarielle said as they finally kissed and became man and wife.

# WE'RE BETTER TOGETHER

*Prologue*

Thirteen-year-old Kaia Kelly, with her beautiful red hair and hazel brown eyes, and her family had lived in Leeside all her life. Within that time, her family had become best friends with the Davis family and had been so since she could remember.

Her family consisted of Ella, Kaia's snotty older s ister; Leroy, her adorable younger brother; and her parents. The Davis family consisted of Molly, Holden, Irene, Kendal, Eloise, and their parents, Mr. and Mrs. Davis.

All of these children were quite attractive, but they all looked quite different.

Ella Kelly had blonde hair and shallow blue eyes, and Molly Davis had brown hair and hazel eyes, and they were very close friends. If possible, they were even closer now than when they were younger because now that they were sixteen, they could go on double dates together.

Irene had gorgeous yellow blonde hair and blue eyes and Kendel had brown hair and hazel eyes. They were Kaia's best friends. Unlike Ella and Molly, these three girls were all different ages—Irene was eleven while Kendal was nine.

Leroy Kelly, with his dirty blonde hair and deep blue eyes, and Eloise Davis with her brown bob and hazel brown eyes, were both five. They were always together while everyone else was in school, and enjoyed playing with each other almost every day. You couldn't separate them for anything.

Last, but certainly not least (in Kaia's mind, at least), is thirteen-year-old Holden Davis. He was charming; he had brown hair and amazing, deep-ocean-blue eyes. He didn't have someone of the same gender like everyone else had in the Kelly family, but he was always hanging with everyone and spreading the love.

The person he was closest to though, was Kaia. They were even closer than everyone in the whole world's closeness combined, if possible. If you stick around, you'll find out why.

The moms of these two families, Mrs. Kelly and Mrs. Davis, had been planning an early Christmas present for all the girls. All the girls were included except for little Eloise because, in her own words, she "wanted to stay and play with Leroy instead of being with the boring older people, even if that means I'll be surrounded by boys for a week."

The mothers and girls of the two families were going on a big trip, to India to serve the locals and to celebrate a most unusual Christmas, in "the most beautiful place," according to Kaia, the history lover. They were going to spend Christmas morning in and around the magnificent Taj Mahal.

Once the girls returned, the dads and boys of the families would be going to have their own trip to Florida to go hunting and fishing.

*Chapter 1*

"Ella, Kaia! Wake up! Breakfast is ready! You don't want to miss your bus!" Mrs. Kelly yelled to her children upstairs.

"Already here, Mom, you don't have to yell!" Ella yelled back at her from the table two feet away.

"Where's Kaia?" her mother asked.

"Mom, do you *really* have a brain that's *that* forgetful? She's doing what she does every morning. She is, very annoyingly, waking up Leroy with her annoying 'hide and seek' game." said Ella with an attitude.

"It's not annoying, it's cute and the perfect way to show love to a younger sibling," said Mrs. Kelly with an affectionate smile on her face as she sat in her own seat at the table.

Meanwhile, in a little room down the hall from the dining room, Kaia was doing her little "hide and seek" game with Leroy, her precious little brother who was her biggest fan, next to Holden, that is.

"I wonder where he is? Where are you, Leroy? Are you under the bed?" Kaia asked as she eagerly looked under the little bed. "Nope, not here. Hmm, maybeeee…. he's in the closet!" she said slowly and then fast as she thoroughly searched her brother's closet.

"No, no," came the sweetest little voice from the bed, "Kaia, I'm right here!" The voice finished while laughing uncontrollably.

"Oh, I see. You're behind the curtain then?" Kaia asked as she looked behind the bright blue curtains that didn't match the sunny yellow room.

"No, I'm in my bed, my big boy bed."

Kaia laughed at how Leroy had to be so specific with his new birthday bed instead of the old crib she and her siblings had used.

"You're in your bed? Your big boy bed? Wow, that must mean your five? Tell me, are you five?"

"Kaia, you remember, don't you? I turned five yesterday and now I'm a big boy. You gave me a bike helmet, remember?" Leroy said worriedly because he thought his most favorite person in the whole world had forgotten his "most important birthday," as he called it.

"Don't worry, I didn't forget, Big Boy Leroy." Kaia answered with Leroy's "new big boy name," also as he liked to call it. "I mean, how could I have forgotten your 'most important birthday'?" She asked, sitting in front of her brother. "Talking about your birthday, friends are coming over today, and you need to help Mom get ready while Ella and I are at school."

"Yes, I will be a good helper, a good big boy helper. Do you think Mom will let me help frost the cake and get out the ice cream all by myself?"

"Maybe, if you are the good helper you say you'll be, but you'll have to ask her, not me."

"Kaia! Come on, I'm starving, and I don't want to miss the bus!" yelled Ella from the dining room.

"Coming!" Kaia called back, then to Leroy, "get on my shoulders, Big Boy Leroy."

"Yes! I love being on your shoulders, it's so much fun!"

◎◎◎

Hours later, after Ella and Kaia had got home from school, the doorbell sounded, "ding-dong, ding-dong."

"I wonder who that could be? Do you know who it is, Leroy?" said Mrs. Kelly with a big, kind smile on her face.

"FRIENDS!" he shouted loud enough to be heard streets away as he opened the front door.

"Mom," said Ella, "can you keep him quiet for once?" then, right after, "Molly! We have so much to plan for tomorrow," she said loudly enough, guiding her teenage friend to her teenage room.

"Leroy!" shouted another little voice.

"Eloise! You came!" Leroy shouted back even though his friend was right in front of him.

"I picked this out all by myself just for you, Leroy, it's a race car, a blue race car!" said little Eloise, who was already in love with the little boy.

"Eloise!" her sister Irene scolded. "He's supposed to open it and find out what it is for himself, remember?"

"Oh, yeah, sorry Leroy. I was just so excited to give it to you," apologized Eloise, a little sad now.

"It's okay, but now I get to open it up already knowing what it is, and then we can play cars!" Leroy, always the happy one, said excitedly to Eloise.

"Can we ask if it is cake time? I'm hungry for cake right now." Eloise said.

"So am I, let's go ask," said Leroy.

While this little exchange was happening, Kaia, Irene and Kendal were also exchanging excited greetings.

"Aren't you excited for the girls' trip tomorrow and the rest of the week, too?" asked Kaia excitedly.

"Are you kidding?" Irene said. "Kendal, Molly, and I have been packing non-stop the entire week!"

"It's true. We've packed, then unpacked, and packed again to make sure we had everything, and we didn't forget anything." said Kendal enthusiastically. Although she was the youngest, she held her own with her friends.

"I know, and now I'll finally be able to say I've been out of the United States *plus* been on an airplane," Kaia said proudly. "Now let's go get some cake and ice cream before it's all gone, 'cause trust me, it will disappear fast with Dad around."

◉◉◉

While eating the deliciousness of chocolate cake and strawberry ice cream, Kaia spoke up. "I just remembered, I have a surprise for you."

"A surprise for me! Yay! You always give the best presents like the bike helmet you gave me yesterday," said Leroy in a very excited voice.

"No, no," said Kaia laughing, "I have a surprise for Irene and Kendal." While turning back to her friends, she finished saying, "It's a book about Ancient India so we can have a little bit more knowledge about the country while we're there this week."

"Sweet. I can't wait to read it and find out all about Ancient India while you're in modern-day India," said a male voice right behind them as he took the book out of Kaia's hands and started flipping through the pages.

"You scared me, and you are not taking it, Holden," said Kendal, as she took the book from her brother's grasp and gave it back to her friend.

"I guess I won't," said Holden sadly. "I bet it will give you lots of needed information to go to modern-day India, but hey, maybe it won't, and then I could feel like I'm there myself," he finished teasingly.

"Holden, please stop." said Irene to her brother, "Sometimes you can actually be pleasant. Can't you be so now?"

"Whoa, sorry to burst your bubble." Holden said, stepping back and putting his hands up like a shield, "I just want to know how history helps the modern-day world?" he said, looking at Kaia with a wondering, knowing glance.

"Holden," Kaia said, "History is helpful in the modern-day world because it helps us know how we got to this day and what has happened before us. It also shows what life would be like without modern-day inventions. Meaning history does help us now and it will, forever. Also, without history we would not be where we are right now. We would not exist, as you should know because of your very sciency mind." Kaia said, obviously annoyed because she had had this conversation with her friend before.

"I guess that kind of makes sense, but not really. Well, I'll leave history to you because you understand it and appreciate it way more than *I* do," finished Holden.

"And I'll leave Science to you because you understand that better than I do," said Kaia.

"You both realize that without science, we wouldn't understand history, and without history, we wouldn't understand science very well, right?" said Kendal with a confused look.

"Yes, we realize." Holden and Kaia said at the same time, looking far into each other's eyes.

Now, Holden and Kaia had been in the same grade at school since before kindergarten. They had always had subjects they did well—their specialties—and ones they didn't do so well—their weaknesses.

And while one was good at something, it turned out the other wasn't so good at that… and vice versa. Because of this they always helped each other with their homework and they worked well together.

Each of them had only one secret the other didn't know about the other. For both of them, it was that they had the biggest crush on the other, and when I say big, I mean gigantic, humongous.

"Can we finish eating now, please?" asked Kendal as
Holden went all the way to his seat.

Once he was there, Irene said teasingly, "Ooo, someone
likes Holden." as she elbowed Kaia sitting next to her.

"No, I don't," Kaia said defensively. "Okay, yes, I like
him, but strictly as a friend and no more than that."

"Are you positively sure about that?" Kendal asked.
"Yes, I'm perfectly sure." Kaia snapped back.

"Looks like someone woke up on the wrong side of the
bed this morning," said Kendal, laughing.

"Sorry, I didn't mean it like that. Can we just change the
subject, please?" asked Kaia.

Now, what the girls didn't know was that Holden was
eavesdropping and loved the way Kaia was handling it.
She was upset with the subject about the two of them,
and that must mean she liked him, which made him happy.

*Chapter 2*

"Kaia, Irene, Kendal, Ella, Molly!" called Mrs. Kelly up
the stairs, "Come on, we're leaving in half an hour!"

"Right here, again, Mom!" said Ella just as loudly, then,
quieter now, "Hey Mom? I have a question."

"Yes, what is it, sweet?" asked Mrs. Kelly.

"I probably should have asked you this earlier, but I
don't think Kaia, Irene, and Kendal should go. I think Dad
and Mr. Davis should go instead," said Ella quickly.

"Now, why would you think that?" asked Mrs. Kelly.
"They have been more excited about this trip than you and
Molly have, especially your sister. You know it is her dream to
go to India sometime, and now's her chance."

"Yes, I know, Mom," said Ella nervously, "but the dads
are already packed because of their trip to Florida. And, just
like Kaia said, the Taj Mahal is such a beautiful and romantic

place. It would be perfect for you and Dad, and Mr. and Mrs. Davis. Also, this would give Molly and me more time to be together instead of babysitting Kaia and her baby friends on the trip."

"What? Of course not. A week is a long time for six children to be parentless." Mrs. Kelly said worriedly.

"But Mom, there's only four children. Holden and Kaia are teenagers now." Ella said, "And you know Kaia's always wanting to babysit, and now's her chance when I'm gone. Please, Mom, will you think about it?"

"Alright, let me go talk to the other parents, but no guarantees, got it?" Mrs. Kelly said as she walked away from her oldest daughter.

Outside, at the back of the truck, Kaia, Irene, and Kendal were helping Holden arrange all the bags in the truck.

"I wonder what the parents could be talking about in there?" Kendal said, looking into the house and seeing all the parents having a kind of heated conversation.

"I bet the moms are just making sure the dads can care for three children for an entire week," answered Holden.

"Oh, Holden, they know perfectly well that the dads are capable of taking care of their children. But I'm not so sure that they'll be able to take care of your wild self," said Kendal as she hurriedly ran out of reach of him.

"Very funny, Kendal." Holden said back. "I still think they're making sure the dads know what to do. I mean, Dad is never home to take care of us."

"I don't know, but I bet it's really important." Kaia said softly. "Well, they're coming over here now, so I'm sure we'll find out soon enough."

"Kaia, Holden, how do you guys feel about being parents for a week?" asked Mrs. Kelly, "You are a good pair, I've got to admit."

Moving away from Holden and her Mom, Kaia said, "First of all, the joke about Holden and I is not funny. *AT ALL.* Second, I won't be here this week. I'm going on the trip, remember?"

"Sweet, you and Holden might have to act like parents this week. The other parents and I had a discussion, and we feel it is best for us, plus the older girls, to go to India while you three younger girls stay here. But we promise to make it up to you when we get back, okay?" said Mrs. Kelly.

"Okay," Kaia said coldly, as she grabbed her bag and stomped inside.

Holden stayed silent during this exchange and was still quiet as he grabbed the other girls' bags and replaced them with the dad's bags.

While Holden was doing this, Mrs. Kelly went inside to talk to Kaia about meals, bedtime, activities, and more for the week. Then, she made sure Kaia and Holden both had phones and emergency numbers and helpful adult contacts.

◉◉◉

All at once the parents and older girls were gone on their adventure to India with Kaia left at home, crying her heart out on her bed. Kaia had been so looking forward to the trip and being at the Taj Mahal, forever it seemed like, but now it wasn't happening, not yet anyway. It better happen later, she thought. Besides, she still had the Ancient India book to find all about India even if it wasn't true about India nowadays and she had already read it many times.

Around five, Kaia went downstairs and started preparing dinner, tomato soup, and grilled cheese sandwiches. Holden came and helped but was quiet until they were almost done, "Kaia," he said, "I'm sorry for making it so you couldn't go to India, it was my idea. I gave the idea to Ella, and of course, the idea thrilled her, going on a trip you had set your heart on without you. I just felt like you, Irene, and Kendal weren't supposed to go, and apparently, that's how the parents feel, too. But if I would have known what the outcome would be, I never would have suggested it."

While Holden talked, Kaia got redder and redder. "Holden, how could you," she exploded. "I've been looking forward to that trip for months and months, then, all of a sudden, I'm stuck here with you instead of there!"

Then, right as Holden was about to speak again, Kaia called, "Dinner!" then, quietly to Holden, "Don't talk about it again."

*Chapter 3*

The week Kaia had, at least with her friends, was amazing. No parents to tell them what to do, lots of ice cream from the freezer, plus games and movies galore. But, on Christmas morning, everyone was in the best spirits they had been all week. It was Christmas, and the next day their parents would be home!

Everyone woke up around five o'clock to the two toddlers yelling, "WAKE UP! WAKE UP! Santa came!" and, "PRESENTS! PRESENTS! PRESENTS!"

"Coming, coming. You can stop yelling now," Kaia said as she slowly walked down the stairs.

"Are you making pancakes? Special sprinkle goodie pancakes with eggnog, Kaia?" asked sweet little Leroy.

"Special sprinkle goodie pancakes with eggnog?" asked Kendal.

"Yes, we have them every Christmas, and it's *soooo* good," answered Leroy.

"If you think they're good, then they must be because you have a sweet tooth," Holden said to Leroy as he patted the little boy's head.

"They are so good," Leroy said enthusiastically. "What is a sweet tooth? Is it something the tooth fairy gives you?" he asked.

"It means you like sugar, and no, the tooth fairy doesn't give it to you," said Holden, trying to control his laughter. "Now why don't we go help your sister with those pancakes you were talking about."

After some stirring, pouring, and flipping, there were delicious pancakes on the table with Leroy using his "big boy voice" yelling, "BREAKFAST! BREAKFAST! BREAKFAST!"

"But I thought we were doing presents first," said a disappointed Eloise as she sat down at the table.

"We're eating first, then we can find out what Santa brought us, okay?" Irene said.

"Okay," said Eloise.

Once everybody was done eating, Leroy was the first one to the living room and the presents. "Now can we open the presents up?" he asked as everybody filed in behind him.

"There's a big one here for everybody. Why don't we all help unwrap it," said Kaia as everybody got to work unwrapping the gigantic present.

Once it was unwrapped, Kaia found a note in between all the wrapped presents inside the big present. She read it aloud: "'Dear kids, we decided to give you these presents because we wanted to give you all something you will remember. Something made by us. We hope you love them because we loved making them and love you all very much. Love, your parents.' OK, now we can open all the presents up but in an orderly fashion. Everyone opens their present from their parents first, then it's the next person's turn. Eloise, do you want to open up your present first?" asked Kaia.

"I'd be happy to," said Eloise as she grabbed her present from the box and opened it. "A doll!" she said excitedly. "And a tag! What does it say?"

"It says 'To Eloise, Love, Mom.' Leroy, would you like to go next?" asked Kaia.

"Of course," he said as he ripped the wrapping paper off his present. "Yippee! A wooden car! It has a tag too, what does it say?"

"'Leroy #1, To Leroy, Love Dad.' Kendal?"

"It's a doll, and the tag says 'To Kendal, Love Mom.'" Kandal read her note.

"Irene, your turn," Kaia said.

"Yes," said Irene as she carefully opened up her gift from her parents. "I got a doll too, and my note says, 'To Irene, Love Mom.'"

"Now, I'll open up mine, and then it is your turn, Holden," Kaia said Holden's name just as coldly as she had done all week long. "My doll's tag says 'To Kaia, love Mom.'"

Then Holden opened his gift very slowly, and as he pulled out a wooden toy car he read his note, "'Holden #1, To Holden, Love, Dad.'"

"Let's move onto the gifts from Santa.  Eloise, do you want to open yours?" Kaia then asked.

*Chapter 4*

That night, their parents and older sisters were supposed to come home. Because of this everyone went to bed with a smile on their face, everyone, that is, except Kaia.

She couldn't help feeling that something wasn't right, and it kept her up all night. Finally, around midnight, she got up and went into the kitchen. She fixed herself something to eat, then started reading her book.

A couple of minutes later there was a knock at the door. Kaia thought it strange that someone was knocking at the door in the middle of the night. She silently walked to the window and looked out. She immediately saw the police car and opened the door.

"Aunt Suzie? What are you doing here?"

"Well, it isn't on good terms, if that's what you're wondering. I came here to tell you some bad news, and I'm sorry I came so late," said the officer, who happened to be Kaia's aunt Suzie.

"What is it? Oh, sorry, I forgot my manners, come in, please." Kaia said as she gave her aunt a big hug and led her to the couch.

"Well, first, I need to know if your brothers are here. Are they?"

"Yes, they are."

"Are your friends Holden, Irene, Kendal, and Eloise Davis here?"

"Yes, they are here, too. Is everything okay? Are we part of the problem? I thought you knew they were here? What's going on? Why are you here in the middle of the night?" Kaia fired off fast.

"Whoa," Aunt Suzie said. "I'll answer all your questions, but I need to talk to Holden too. Will you wake him up, please?" she asked.

"Of course, I'll go get him."

◉◉◉

Down the hall, in Leroy's room, Holden was snoring away. Kaia found him and shook him awake. "Holden, wake up. My Aunt, Aunt Suzie, the police officer. She's here, and I think something is wrong. She says she needs to talk to us both." Kaia whispered fast.

"What? Why?" Holden asked, not so quietly.

"Shh, I don't know yet, but we'll find out faster if you would just get up."

"Why would she come this late? How did you hear the knock? I didn't."

"I couldn't fall asleep, so I went to the kitchen to read so I wouldn't wake up the girls. Now get up, lazy head, Aunt Suzie is waiting."

"Who's calling me a lazy head? Demanding human being."

"Oh," Kaia said while suppressing a quiet giggle. "Now look who's calling other people names, *Annoying Leetle Colden*," said Kaia, using her friend's old nickname, the one she had given him when they were toddlers and just learning to talk. "Now come on, she's waiting."

"Oh, so I'm *Annoying Leetle Colden* again, am I, Crazy Preetty Kaiy," said Holden, using Kaia's old nickname.

"I'm *Crazy Preetty Kaiy* again too, am I?"

"Apparently you are," Holden replied, also quietly laughing, looking up and right into Kaia's beautiful hazel eyes.

◎◎◎

Back in the living room, Aunt Suzie was looking at the wall of family pictures and heard Kaia and Holden sharing that quiet laugh. This pleased her; she knew their parents had wanted them to be a match someday.

"Here we are. Now, what did you want to talk to us about?" asked Kaia with a smile on her face, pleased she and Holden were on good terms again.

"Well, it's kind of a touchy subject, so I'll just go right out and say it. Your parents and older sisters are dead," Aunt Suzie said, very unsympathetically to Kaia's ears.

"What?" the girl said, starting to tear up. "No, th-they're supposed to come home today. They can't be dead."

"How did it happen?" Holden asked. "They were supposed to be on a plane flying home right now."

"Well, instead of taking the more expensive, more secure plane, they took a small plane. While on the plane, they flew into a dangerous storm, and the plane didn't make it to its destination. That's all I know," Aunt Suzie said.

"Th-they can't be dead." All at once, Kaia started sobbing, "I-it could have been me. It should have been me."

"No, it shouldn't have been you," Holden said. "I get it now. That's why I felt so strongly that you and Irene and Kendal shouldn't have gone. It all makes perfect sense now."

Holden comforted Kaia as Aunt Suzie left. "By giving the idea to Ella of you all staying here, you are alive and healthy, same with my sister. Well, three of them at least."

Kaia stopped crying for a minute to say, "Holden, y-you saved my life, a-along with Irene and Kendal. Thank you. Thank you so much." Then she started bawling all over again. "Thank you so very much. But if we did go, you, Leroy, and Eloise would at least still have the dad's, but now you have no one. There's no one left except for us."

87

"Kaia, please don't blame yourself, it's not your fault."

After Holden said that, he held Kaia while she cried her heart out, as he tried to keep his tears back. They sat like that for a long time, until Kaia finally fell asleep and the sun started coming up.

What Holden didn't know was that two mischievous girls were standing in the hallway where his line of sight could not reach.

"Come on, we should leave before he sees us. We have been here for, like, five minutes already, let's go," Kendal whispered as she pulled on her sister's arm.

"Just one more moment, Kendal, please," Irene whispered without looking at her.

"Why are they like that anyway? And where are our parents? Shouldn't they be back by now?" asked Kendal, with more than a tint of worry in her voice.

"I don't know," Irene whispered. "I think something's wrong. It looks like they have been crying."

"Okay, come on, let's go, anyway," Kendal whispered. "We have been out here long enough. Whatever they're doing is none of our business anyway. Come on," she whispered as she gently pulled Irene back to Kaia's room.

After they had gone, Holden put Kaia on the couch and covered her with a blanket. Then he started making breakfast cake for breakfast, Kaia's favorite, even though he hated it himself.

*Chapter 5*

The smell of the delicious breakfast cake filled the house and, one by one, everyone came out and sat at the table, waiting to eat. Holden then offered the prayer and everyone dug in.

Only then, did Irene start trying to figure out what she and Kendal saw earlier that morning.

"Where's Kaia?" she asked innocently enough, "She wasn't in bed when we woke up this morning."

"She's asleep on the couch," was Holden's short reply as Kendal gave Irene a warning look. She knew exactly where her sister was and what she was doing, or trying to do anyway.

"Why'd she sleep there instead of in her bed?" Irene continued prying.

"She couldn't sleep last night, so she came out here so she wouldn't bother you and Kendal."

"How do you know that?"

"I'm sorry, but I refuse to answer that question," Holden said very calmly even though he was not so close to being so calm inside. There was so much more to talk about, besides Kaia being asleep on the couch.

"So, either you don't know, or you're just not going to tell us. I personally think it's the second one, after what Kendal and I saw this morning with you and Kaia."

By now, Leroy and Eloise were both silent too, and actually interested, even though they had no idea what the older kids were talking about.

Holden was the only one not interested now.

Comforting Kaia was his and Kaia's business alone right now, at least. No one else's, no matter how hard other people tried to make it theirs.

"You were holding Kaia while she slept, why?" Irene said as Holden's cheeks got redder and redder, and angrier and angrier. "We already know you and Kaia are best friends and have crushes on each other. We also already know the parents have already planned your wedding and everything. But that was a little bit too much too fast."

Holden took a deep breath. "Yes, Kaia is my best friend, and yes, I do think she is very beautiful indeed. No, I did not know that our parents have already planned our wedding, and that wedding will most likely not happen. And the reason I was holding her the way I was was because she needed comfort. Now, this discussion is over." He was surprisingly calm, but on the bitter side toward the two girls, as he stood up to wash the dishes.

"So, where are our parents" Aren't they supposed to be home by now?" Irene asked in a haughty way.

"Why do you have so many questions this morning, Irene? And I don't know exactly where the parents are. I haven't received a call from them since they called us to say goodnight yesterday," Holden said. Although extremely angry now, he was proud of himself for not having told a lie through all the explanations he had had to give so far. Knowing Irene, he didn't know how long he could keep that up.

"Holden," said Eloise in her little-girl voice. What's wrong? You're angry, and you're never angry."

"Eloise, you and everyone here are safe, so I am happy," said Holden, calming down to his sisters' sweetness.

"Okay. I love you," Eloise said, then gave him a quick kiss.

"I love you too, and so does Mommy and Daddy," said Holden, with a faraway look in his eyes.

That's the moment Kaia decided to wake up. "Morning everyone. Yum, what smells so good?"

"Breakfast cake!" yelled all four different voices at once.

"Just for you," said another voice, Holden's voice. Kaia knew Holden hated breakfast cake… Weird right? But Kaia knew exactly why he had made it, even if he disliked it very much.

"Mmm, that sounds delicious," was Kaia's reply, with a warm smile.

"Holden's been acting very strange, and he doesn't know where our parents are. Can you tell us?" asked Kendal.

"He's been acting strange, how?"

"He's angry, and you know he's never angry," said Eloise.

"Hmm. I do know he's never angry."

"Now, will you please tell us where our parents are? Please?" asked Kandal.

"Welllll," Kaia said, dragging out the word as she looked at Holden.

"I didn't say anything, I promise, what I did say was the truth," Holden said with his hands up defensively.

"Something funny is going on here, and I would like to know what it is," Irene said, looking back and forth between her brother and friend.

"Kaia, where are Mom and Dad? I'm scared." Leroy said as he tugged on her sleeve.

"I'm scared too, they haven't been here for a long time, and Holden said he doesn't know where they are," said Eloise.

"Yeah, where are they?" Kendal asked.

"I want Mommy and Daddy!" cried Leroy.

Kaia got on her knees and held the two five-year-olds as they cried, knowing they would be crying even more later when they found out that their parents wouldn't be coming home, that they were, in fact, lying at the bottom of the Pacific Ocean.

"Don't worry, Holden and I, will tell you what's going on, just not right now, okay? Let me at least get some yummy food in my tummy first."

◎◎◎

Everyone finished their breakfast, got their snow clothes on, and walked to the snow-covered park. On the way, Holden and Kaia walked in the back in companionable silence, knowing the other one was in pain because of the truth, too.

At the park, they sat and talked about school, the most boring subject to talk about during Christmas break. Then when Irene and Kendal came over, Kaia left to play with the little kids. She left because she knew why they were coming over, and she did not want to be a part of that conversation.

## Chapter 6

That night, Kaia and Holden told everyone else that their parents would not be returning. Aunt Suzie stopped by, again in her police officer's uniform, as evidently this was official business. She told them that they needed to decide if they wanted to live with relatives or go to an orphanage and foster parents.

Then Kendal had an idea, "What if we stayed here, in this house, together. I mean, the Kelly's weren't renting this house, they own it."

"Yes, I guess you could, but then you will have to find a way to provide for each other and keep each other safe. Holden, if you are willing to find a job to support everyone, and Kaia, if you are willing to take care of everyone by cooking, cleaning, and caring for the others as a mom would, and the rest of you are willing to care for each other as we-"

"Yes, we are." interrupted Kaia. "At least I would be willing to do whatever I need to to keep us together. But I don't know about the rest of you," she said, turning to look at the others.

"Yes, we are," said Holden, Irene, and Kendal at the same time, eager to stay within their own family.

"Alrighty then, I'll come here once a week to check on you. If you aren't taking care of each other as you should, well…" Aunt Suzie paused. "You still might have to decide if you would rather go to relatives or an orphanage." With that, she left.

"Now," Kaia said, "if we want to stay together, we need to work together as Aunt Susie said. School starts tomorrow, but the school is giving us a week to sort ourselves out, so let's get into a good schedule this week. Holden, you need to find a job, and I will, too. Then we need to find a way to get places. Let's start with that and go on from there."

◉◉◉

During the week, Holden got a good-paying job, good-paying at least for a thirteen-year-old, at the local grocery store. Kaia also was hired for a good-paying job for a thirteen-year-old, at the library. And they all worked out a good schedule of helping each other with all the chores and things around the house.

Everyone went back to school once the week was over. Holden and Kaia were only in eighth grade, Irene in fifth, Kendal in fourth, and Eloise and Leroy started kindergarten.

Kaia's first class was English, her all-time favorite class. She would even choose it as a favorite over Social Studies, and that's saying something. She loved it because she loved writing. She loved writing stories about everything from the past to the present, to the future, but mostly about the past and the present.

"Kaia, I'm so sorry about yours and Holden's parents. Are you all alright? Is there anything I can do?" asked Mrs. Pena, Kaia's favorite teacher, who was the English teacher.

"I'm good, and, no, there's nothing you can do," Kaia answered, trying not to cry about the overall subject.

"Are you sure? Losing your parents and older sibling is hard. Just let me know if you need anything, okay?"

"Yes, ma'am, I will, and again, thank you."

"Boys, stop fighting this instant." Mrs. Pena said as she left the room to talk to some students who were fighting in the hall.

"Well, look who's back, it's the teacher's pet, Miss Kaia Kelly," said a jealous voice.

"Leave me alone, Micah," Kaia responded.

"Aren't you supposed to be home crying about your parents on Holden's shoulder while he cries about his?" Micah said as she found yet another way to tease Kaia about Holden.

"I told you to stop," said Kaia with tears in her eyes.

"You're a baby, and your parents weren't very smart to go on that trip. Just admit that you like Holden for once, go on, you wouldn't be lying, we all know that."

"Holden's like my brother. Why would I like him in the way you're suggesting. Don't say anything against my parents. They were people who loved me just the way I am."

Just as Micah was about to speak, her face inches from Kaia's, Mrs. Pena walked in then.

"Kaia, Micah, what's going on?" she asked as she saw Kaia's face in her hands.

"I was just trying to be nice. All I did was tell her I was sorry about what happened to her and Holden's parents. Then she started bawling," then more quietly, so only Kaia could hear, "like a baby."

"Is this true, Kaia?"

"Yes, it is ma'am," Micah's best friend, Laura, said before Kaia could say anything.

"Well, let's get to work then, shall we?" Mrs. Pena said. "Everyone, get out your notebooks, we will be doing creative writing today," she said as she winked at Kaia, knowing it was Kaia's favorite thing to do, and that she was good at it too.

Down the hall and to the right, in Mr. Jenning's classroom, the same kind of thing was happening to Holden, but this time, in his least favorite class, math.

"Well, well, well. Look who's back, Holden Davis. I just hope you and Kaia are not stupid like your parents," said Finley Bagleys, the school bully.

Holden jumped up and grabbed Finley. "Kaia is not stupid, and neither were our parents."

"Oh, so I see you defend Kaia, but not yourself. You know, I hope you don't get Kaia and yourself killed someday because you admitted that you're stupid. And it would be a shame if you got Kaia killed because she is the school beauty, with her fiery red hair. I would just love to touch it," Finley said just to make Holden mad.

"I suggest you stop talking right now, Finley, or you'll be sorry. And her red hair is not for you to touch. No one is to touch it, not on my watch."

"Holden, Finley, what's going on?" asked Mr. Jennings as he walked into the room.

"Mr. Jennings, help me, Holden's holding me against my will," Finley lied.

"You're a liar and a coward." Holden spit out as their teacher pulled them apart.

"Now, Holden, I know you're having a hard time without your parents, but that is not an excuse to let your anger out on other students." Then, to the whole class this time, "Why are you all out of your seats? Sit down and start working on your math lesson. Holden, you'll have to catch up on the things you missed."

◎◎◎

Later at lunch, Kaia and Holden sat across from each other at the end of a back table where they always sat in the cafeteria.

"I heard Micah wasn't very nice to you in first-hour," said Holden as he took a bite of his meatloaf.

"No, she wasn't, but when is she ever nice?"

"Good one," Holden said, laughing.

"What are they laughing about over there?" Finley asked his "best friend" Bert.

"I don't know," Bert answered.

"Well, no matter what, I will find a way to get her to like me because she is the prettiest girl in the school, and I'm the most popular. So really, she should be begging me to take her to the Valentine's Day dance, just to get her new friends and get her to be popular, through me. I mean, look, she needs new friends. That Holden is a baby."

"You're going to ask her to the Valentine's Day dance?"

"Of course. Don't you have faith in me? Just watch the pro do it." Finley said as he walked over to Kaia and sat down right next to her.

"Hey beauty, do you want to go to the Valentine's Day dance with the most popular kid in the school?" Finley asked, with his thumb rubbing her cheek.

Kaia visibly shook but stayed quietly eating her lunch. When Holden saw Finley touching Kaia, he jumped up, grabbed Finley's hand away from Kaia, and twisted it hard.

"Ow! Stop hurting me!"

"Don't ever touch her again, or I will hurt you worse," Holden said, through clenched teeth.

"Holden, it's okay, you can let go now," Kaia said calmly. Then to Finley, once Holden released him, she said, "First of all, my name is not 'Beauty,' it's Kaia, Kaia Kelly to you. Second of all, you're not the most popular kid in the school, just the meanest. Oh sorry, you were talking about yourself when you asked, if I wanted to go with the most popular kid in school, right? I will not go to a dance or on a date until I am at least sixteen, and even then I won't go with certain people even if they ask me."

This was like a slap across Finlay's face.

Holden had the biggest smile on now, obviously proud of Kaia. "You heard her, she won't go with you, now go."

"You like this unsmart, plain-looking, rude weirdo, don't you, Kaia? I can't believe you'd choose him over me, who could give you popularity while he can give you absolutely nothing." Finley said as he stood up and walked away.

Once he was gone, Kaia said, "Thank you, Holden."

"What are you thanking me for? You were awesome! You said no to him, and I don't think anybody has ever said no to him before."

"Ya, I guess I did, but you got rid of him," Kaia said.

"I guess I did help, but only a little. But, still, the way you told him no was incredible!"

## Chapter 7

Years passed and surprisingly, they were able to stay together. In fact, all the kids grew even closer together than they ever were before they were one big happy family. They went on family vacations from places like amusement parks to the ocean.

Kaia was still a librarian, which she loved because of the peace, along with all the books. Even though she wanted to be an author when she was older, being around other authors' masterpieces was one of her favorite things.

Holden, on the other hand, was no longer working at the grocery store. He was a scientist's apprentice, which he loved, but he also loved Kaia.

Since they were now 17 and in twelve grade, Holden had asked Kaia to go with him to prom, and she had said yes! The other girls—Irene, Kendal, and Eloise—were dressing Kaia up for prom that night.

"You should wear this dress." said Eloise, now nine years old. She held up a beautiful white dress with lace all over it.

"No, she shouldn't, not tonight. She should wear that when she gets married to Holden," said Kendal. "She should wear this red dress that matches her hair."

"I agree that Kaia should wait wear to white one until they are married, but I think the red one is too matchy with her hair," said Irene.

"I'm not ever getting married to Holden," Kaia said. "This is just a friendly dance that we're going to."

"Oh, trust me, you'll marry him someday, and the gorgeous white lace dress will be reserved specifically for it," Irene responded.

"How about she wears this one," said Kendal as she held up the most beautiful green dress that went well with Kaia's hair perfectly.

"Oh, yeah. It'll be beautiful on her," said the girls at once.

"Put it on, I want to see you in it," said Kendal excitedly.

"All right," Kaia said as she changed into the beautiful green dress.

"Yes, you should wear it. No, you n*eed* to wear it."

"It looks like it was made just for you."

"That green is the most stunning color with your hair."

"You'll be the most beautiful girl on the dance floor, that's for sure."

"If Holden's not in love with you all ready, then he will be tonight."

"Thank you for all the compliments," Kaia said, blushing a little. "And by the way, Holden is not in love with me nor will he ever be," she added defensively.

"Stop acting like he doesn't like you and you don't like him! We already know the truth," Eloise said as she pulled Kaia to the chair.

"Now, what should we do with your hair?" Kendal asked, mostly to herself.

"I know, we should do braids and then wrap them around her head into that really cool bun thing!" Eloise answered excitedly.

"Yes, that's perfect!" Irene said.

"Let's hurry, though. I think the boys are almost ready," Irene said.

"Oh, let them wait. Holden will thank us later when he sees Kaia," Kendal said as she got to work on Kaia's hair.

Once that part of her was as perfect as it could be, the girls worked on Kaia's makeup. They put mascara, blush, eyeshadow, and even a little lipstick on her. Then they were done.

"You're gorgeous, Kaia." Irene said.

"You will definitely soon be our actual sister with the way you look," Kendal said

"Yes, as I said, Holden will fall in love with you tonight if he hasn't already," Irene said in a singsong voice.

"I can't wait to see his face when he sees you," Kendal said excitedly as she clapped her hands in delight.

"Neither can I," said Eloise, just as excitedly.

Just then, there was a knock at the door. "That must be Holden." said Kendal excitedly.

"Your dazzling princess is waiting for you," said Irene as she opened the door all the way so Holden could see Kaia.

One look at Kaia and Holden was speechless. "You're beautiful, Kaia."

"Thank you, and you're very handsome, yourself," Kaia answered as she looked at Holden in his suit. She grabbed his arm, and he steered her downstairs and outside to the car, never looking away from her.

"Wait! We need pictures!" Eloise almost yelled as she grabbed the camera and started snapping away. "Okay, now you can go."

*Chapter 8*

On the way to the school where prom was being held, all Kaia could think about was what the girls had said as they were dressing her up. Did Holden love her? If not, would he fall in love with her tonight?

But all Holden could think about was how beautiful Kaia looked and how beautiful she would look in a white wedding dress, getting married to him.

Once they arrived at the school, Kaia and Holden danced for a long time. Kaia absolutely loved it. She felt so free in Holden's arms and wanted this feeling to stay forever. After a handful of songs, thought, they were both tired and thirsty, so they took a quick break.

"You look so beautiful tonight, you're absolutely stunning, Kaia."

"Thank you, you've already told me, and you're very handsome tonight as well."

"You've already told me that, too," Holden said, chuckling.

"I know, but it's true," she said, matter of factly.

"Just like you're exquisite is," Holden said.

"Thank you," said Kaia with a sweet smile, a little embarrassed.

"Oh, look who's here, Holden and Kaia," a very rude and disrespectful voice said. "I thought you weren't coming, especially together, because you always say you're just like siblings." It was Finley, the old school bully who had tried everything to get Kaia to go out with him; every time Kaia politely declined.

"Go away, Finley," said Kaia as she grabbed Holden's hand and started walking away.

"Why should I? You're not in charge of me, and you're walking away, so how can I." Finley said as he walked up to her and stroked her cheek with his thumb like he did that day in the cafeteria many years earlier.

But this time it was Kaia who grabbed his hand and jerked it around. "If you ever touch me again, it will be worse." Kaia said, very angry now.

"I think he understands now. C'mon, let's go dance some more, Kaia," said Holden, who was angry at Finley too—he had just touched his girl, and Holden would get him back for it.

Holden and Kaia danced for a long time after that, then they took another break and got some more to eat and drink. Then they went outside and walked around for a while, both thinking about the other until she said, "Do you ever miss them?"

For a second, Holden didn't know who Kaia was talking about. "Of course I do, I mean they were my parents and it was my older sister, along with yours."

"I miss them, especially now. You know our parents wanted us to be together, right?"

"Yeah, I remember. And to please them, would you like to go with me on a picnic on Saturday?" Holden asked, grateful for the intro to the question he'd been wanting to ask her.

"You mean, like a date?"

"Yeah, if you want it to be like that, I guess."

"I would love to, but remember what Finley said about us practically being siblings. What would people think then?"

"Don't worry what others will think. Just worry about what I think, along with everyone else in our stitched-together family."

"Okay, then, yes, I would like to go on a picnic date with you," Kaia said with a smile, squeezing his hand.

◎◎◎

After their first so-called date, Kaia and Holden went out once a week on Saturdays. They now called Saturdays date night, and after a few months of this, Holden had a surprise for Kaia.

They had a picnic in the same place they had the first time. They were having a wonderful time eating, surrounded by spring flowers after a long winter.

After some time, Holden stood. "Kaia, I have a question for you, will you please stand up?"

"Okay, what's your question?" Kaia asked as she stood up.

Holden took a deep breath. "Kaia Kelly, you are the most beautiful girl in the whole world. The whole universe. I know we are still young, only eighteen, but I have just one thing to ask of." Now on one knee, he took a red velvet box out of his pocket and opened it. "Kaia, will you marry me?"

The ring was a beautiful band of peachy pearls with "I Love You" engraved onto the inside of the band. It made Kaia cry.

"Holden, how could you want me? Nobody does, I would love to say yes, but we are like siblings and would fight all the time. At least I think so. Please, just let me be alone."

Kaia ran to the house, past the others, and into her room,  the whole time, wiping tears from her face.

Kaia had wanted to say yes, she really did, but she couldn't. Holden and she were the closest friends, more like brother and sister, she wanted to believe, more than anything else. She thought he would get tired of her being his wife instead of siblings all too quickly. She also knew that there was someone out there that would love him more than she ever could... but at the same time, she wasn't sure anyone had loved anyone as much as she loved Holden.

*Chapter 9*

Holden kept trying to talk to Kaia after that, but she wouldn't listen to him. Everyone knew something was wrong because of the way Kaia had come home that day from the forest and how she wouldn't even look at Holden now, even for a second.

"What happened with you and Kaia?" asked Eloise at breakfast one morning while Kaia was getting ready in her room.

"Did you hurt her?" Leroy asked, standing up, ready to defend his sister.

"No, I didn't touch her. All I did was ask a question," Holden said, obviously down.

"Did you ask her to marry you?" Irene asked excitedly.

Holden didn't answer.

"Well, did you?" This time, Eloise had asked.

"Yes, I did, and she said no," Holden answered unhappily.

"Oh, I'm so sorry, Holden," Kendal said with a melancholy tone in her voice.

"Me too." The rest said at the same time.

"It's okay, it's just, I thought she would say yes, but instead, this happens," Holden said.

Just then, there was a knock at the door, and Eloise went to open it. "Good morning, can I help you?"

"Yes, I believe you can. I need to speak with Holden Davis if he is home."

"Yes, he's home. Why don't you come and sit down."

"Good Evening, Dr. Duncan," Holden said as the other person sat down. "What do you need?"

"Well, as you know, I am thinking about moving my laboratory to a city, maybe Chicago or something, and was wondering if you would come along with me," the Doctor said quickly.

"You want me to go to Chicago with you? But what about my family here? I don't want to move them halfway across the United States."

"Well, you wouldn't have to, they could stay here while you move there with me, and you could send them money so they can still survive. Also, if you come along, your paycheck will increase, whereas if you stay here, you will have no job."

"I don't know, I'll have to talk to Kaia about it," Holden replied.

"Well I'm leaving in a week, and you have until then to decide."

As you probably already guessed, Dr. Duncan was the scientist Holden worked for as an apprentice. The doctor had talked about moving his laboratory before, but not so far away, and he hadn't ever mentioned having Holden go with him.

Holden tried to talk to Kaia about the job offer, but when she wouldn't listen, Holden decided that he wanted to go and get away from Kaia for a while. He didn't want to go alone, so he asked Leroy to go with him.

"Leroy, I have a question. Do you want to come to Chicago with me and learn how to become a scientist?" Holden asked.

"Yes, I would like that very much, but what about the girls? Who will stay and look after them?" asked Leroy.

"They are strong, they will look after each other."

"How long will we be gone?"

"I don't know, let's ask Dr. Duncan when he comes later today."

As Holden walked away, Kendal walked up to him, "I want to go, too. You know how I also love science, and I think it would be an amazing experience to help a real-life scientist."

"I don't know Kendal, I mean, I don't even know how long we'll be gone yet."

"Please, I'm sixteen. I am old enough to take care of myself if necessary."

"Fine, I'll think about it."

"Thank you, thank you, thank you!" Kendal said as she gave Holden a big hug.

Dr. Duncan joined them later for dinner. Holden said, "I have decided to go to Chicago with you, Dr. Duncan, but can someone, or even two people, come with me?"

"Well, of course." the scientist said, eyeing Kaia and thinking Holden was talking about her, and maybe the youngest, Eloise.

"I was thinking Leroy right here could come with me, and maybe my sister, Kendal. She wants to be a scientist when she is older," Holden said as he grabbed Leroy's shoulder and pointed to Kendal.

"I thought you were going to bring this pretty young lady with you, as it seems like you will soon be married," Dr. Duncan said, gesturing to Kaia with his hand.

"I am not going, and neither am I ever going to marry this man or any man as a matter of fact," Kaia said very loudly and unhappily, and everyone was surprised.

"Also, Doctor Duncan, how long will we be in Chicago?" asked Leroy, ignoring his sister.

"I don't know, kid, as long as I seem necessary," was the man's reply.

The next day everyone said their goodbyes to Holden, Leroy, and Kendal.

"Goodbye, I hope you have a wonderful time in Chicago!"

"Don't forget about us!"

"Miss you already!"

Everyone yelled to them as they drove, everyone except Kaia, that is. She just went to her room and cried because she wished she could have put things right between her and Holden before he left. Plus Leroy, her adorable little brother and her only real sibling left was now gone, too.

*Chapter 10*

Two years later Holden, Leroy, and Kendal were still in Chicago, at least that's what everyone thought they were. Kaia and the others had not received a phone call, text, letter, or even a check like Holden had promised, since they had left long ago.

In conclusion, Holden and they had either abandoned everyone else, which wasn't very likely at all, or they had completely disappeared.

So now, two years later, Kaia was in college and engaged to Finley Bagleys, who ended up being surprisingly handsome. He had golden-brown hair with milk chocolate brown eyes that went on forever. He was no longer the enemy she remembered from middle and high school. But he wasn't Kaia's Holden—in other words, he wasn't perfect i n Kaia's eyes.

Once Kaia realized Holden wasn't going to be in contact anymore and that they wouldn't receive the money promised from him, she got a better-paying job at the school instead of her librarian job. True, her teaching job didn't pay much, but she loved being around the children.

◉◉◉

On a cold winter night, Kaia had "The Dream" again, the dream that had been haunting her since Holden had proposed, when she had said no, and he disappeared for what seemed like forever.

She heard her name, he was calling her again "Kaia!

Kaia!" He was saying her name over and over. She searched and searched for his voice, but she couldn't find him. It was so irritating!

Finally the voice, his voice sounded close enough, "Kaia! I can't believe it's you! I can't believe I found you!" He was behind her, her beloved childhood friend.

"Holden?" she said, "Holden! I found you!" as they ran into each other's arms.

"Please," he was saying, "let's never be separated again, I love you, Kaia. I love you with all my heart."

"I love you too, Holden," Kaia answered.

Just as they were about to kiss, she woke up. It was just a dream. At first, she was confused, where was he, where was Holden? Where was she?

All at once, she remembered, "Oh, right." she said aloud.

She was in her childhood room, in Leeside. Holden, Leroy, and Kendal were still missing, and she was soon to be married to Finley Bagleys, her old enemy from middle and high school.

Then, out of the blue, the fire alarms in the house started going off.

The alarms were really, very sensitive, meaning every time they cooked in the oven or on the stovetop, they might start. But it was the middle of the night, and no one was using the oven or stove, at least from what she knew.

A second later, Eloise burst into the room, "FIRE!! FIRE!! There's a FIRE!!"

That's all she could say before she ran out of Kaia's room and out of the house with everyone following behind her. Everyone, that is, except Kaia.

◉◉◉

Kaia couldn't breathe. Her lungs were full of smoke. As the fire blazed around her, a burning support beam in the wall decided to fall. Kaia tried to avoid it, but she wasn't fast enough.

"AHHHHH!!" Kaia screamed as it fell on her leg.

Kaia, hurting and exhausted, almost passed out, but she told herself, "Stay awake, stay strong." Over and over again she said this to herself, but finally, she was too exhausted and was hallucinating.

A couple of minutes later, a firefighter picked her up, "Holden?" she said over and over again without realizing what she was saying. And then she fell into a deep, dark coma.

*Chapter 11*

"Is she going to be okay?" Eloise asked.

"Yes, she will be. The burns on her body are quite bad, especially her leg, but in time it will heal. She also breathed in a lot of smoke, but she'll be okay," said the firefighter to the other girls. He had saved Kaia's life.

"Thank you," Irene said, hugging the sobbing Eloise.

"In the meantime, you'll have to find a place to sleep. The house won't be very protective and nice to sleep in now," the firefighter said, gesturing to the smoldering pile of rubbish that used to be their home.

"Yes, we'll find something," Irene said as they watched the ambulance with Kaia inside drive away.

◎◉◎

Meanwhile, in Houston, far away from Chicago, Holden, Leroy, and Kendal had just escaped Doctor Duncan. Instead of taking them to Chicago to learn how to be scientists like he said he would, this evil man had taken them to Houston, Texas to be his slaves.

Yes, they were treated fairly nicely, but they were not allowed any freedoms. Holden was angry, and I mean angry. Dr. Duncan had lied to him and his family about lots of important things—important things, including where they were going and that Holden couldn't send any paychecks back to everyone else, mostly because he didn't get a paycheck.

Now the three of them had finally escaped from the hated Dr. Duncan to go back to where they belong. They belonged in Leeside, with their makeshift family.

Finally, Holden, Leroy, and Kendal traveled home. In the last town before arriving, they saw a paper about a fire in Leeside. The article was about a house burning down. It was about their house burning down, and Kaia with her badly burned body. It said she was still in a coma, over a week later.

After they read the article, they had a reason to get to their home even faster. And that's just what they did.

◎◎◎

In Leeside, in the hospital, in Kaia's room, Finley was sitting next to Kaia, holding her hand. "Wake up, please, Kaia, wake up," he said over and over again.

When the kids were out of school for the day, they also showed up and just watched Kaia as she slept. They watched and waited for any kind of movement, but there was none, none at all.

The next day, Irene went in alone to see Kaia. "Hi Kaia, I know you most likely can hear me, but I just need to talk, and get everything out." Irene started talking about her troubles. When she was done she finished with, "We need you, we need you like we never needed you before. Please wake up, please," and she started crying uncontrollably.

◎◎◎

Holden, Leroy, and Kendal had just arrived in Leeside and were on their way to see the damage to their home.

108

"What if it's nothing but ashes? Where are the others sleeping?" Kendal said with a scared voice.

"They're smart. They've figured something out," Leroy said, pretending not to be worried—but in truth he was worried, too.

Just then they rounded a corner where their home should be—but there was nothing there but ashes.

"It's completely gone. I thought there would be at least something here, at least a little of it left." Holden said, amazed and horrified at the same time. "Come on, let's go find Kaia in the hospital," he said, unable to look at the damage any more.

As they turned away from their former home and started down the lane, they saw two people walking toward them. Out of the blue, the youngest shouted, "Leroy?!" Then started running towards them.

"Eloise?!" Leroy yelled as he ran toward Eloise, and they fell into a big hug.

Then Irene, finally understanding what was going on, shouted, "Holden! Kendal! Leroy!"

"Eloise, is that really you? I can't believe it." Leroy said as he squeezed her even harder.

"Leroy, I thought you forgot about me," Eloise said through tears.

"What, I would never forget about you."

As everyone was giving hugs and saying how much they missed each other, Holden wished Kaia were there.

"Where are you all living now?" Holden asked.

"In a portable home," Irene answered.

"We were just coming here to search through the ashes to see if there is anything left," Eloise said.

"Would you guys like to go see Kaia?" Irene asked, knowing that Holden was dying to see her, consequences or not.

"Yes, please," was Holden's hungry reply.

As they walked toward the hospital, Irene gave Kaia's report, having been the last one there, "She's still unconscious from the burns, and her leg is really painful. At least that's what the doctors are saying." Irene said. "And oh, by the way, Kaia's engaged to your old school enemy."

"She's engaged?! To Finley?!"

"Yep."

*Chapter 12*

Finley was at the hospital, holding Kaia's hand, when the others showed up.

"I didn't think I'd see you here." Finley said as he saw Holden walk into the room. "I thought you abandoned everyone and just disappeared."

"Well, we didn't abandon anyone, and we didn't disappear," Holden said. "I understand that I have to share Kaia with you now."

Oh, we're not sharing her. We are engaged, you know, meaning she is mine, not yours or ours. She is mine, and mine alone."

"And how is it that you got Kaia to say yes to you anyway?"

"She needed a man around the house, is what she said."

"Like she thinks you're a man," Holden shot back.

Finley rolled his eyes, and Holden finally looked at Kaia. He felt like he didn't have a right to sit next to her and hold her hand like Finley was, so he just kept standing and looking at her.

She was so pale, and she looked awful. She must be hurting so much. All Holden wanted to do was take away the pain that was obvious on her face and hold her like he had when they first heard that their parents weren't coming home.

"So, if you didn't disappear or even abandon everyone, then what happened?" Finley asked with fake concern on his face.

"You don't know what Leroy, Kendal, and I went through," was Holden's cold response.

"So, tell us."

"No, thank you," Holden said as he left the room, trying to control his tears.

"He was lied to by his boss. He said we could go work in his laboratory in Chicago with him and that Holden could send paychecks back to help everyone here. But he brought us to Houston as his personal slaves and didn't let us send money back, not that we got any anyway." Leroy said, s queezing Eloise's hand.

Everyone was silent, not expecting that as a response, then they turned to Kendal to confirm what Leroy had said. "It's all true. But let's not talk about that right now."

After everyone left, Holden went back in to see Kaia by himself. This time he did sit by her and hold her hand.

"Kaia," he said, "I don't know if you can hear me, but I'm sorry. I'm sorry.  I thought you would accept me to be your husband. I am sorry I left you so soon after that and took Leroy with me. He is your only real family left, I know.

"I'm also sorry for not trying to contact you for two years, but I physically could not. I'm glad you found some-one you love to be with forever, but I am surprised that person is Finley, to be honest.

"But, please wake up. I want to see you again, and not just in an unconscious state, but where you can see me too. I've deeply missed you, and finally, when I can see you, you're in a coma, unable to move. Please, please wake up." Holden said as he brought her hand to his lips and kissed it.

At that moment, a nurse came into the room, "Visiting hours are over, I need you to leave."

◉◉◉

111

After a few weeks of being back in Leeside and with
Kaia still in a coma, Holden went again to see her by himself.
He sat next to her again, but didn't grab her hand.

"Kaia, I don't know if you can hear me or not, or any of
the other times I've come and talked to you. But, to be truthful, I love you. I love you more than ever, but I'll try to keep
it a brotherly kind of love. I'm glad you have Finley, but, to be
truthful, I still wish you could be mine. Please, I don't want to
be separated like how we were before ever again. But it's kind
of hard to do that when you're asleep like you are."

At this point, he had put their hands together in a high
five, and as he said, "Remember this? Remember when we
were younger, and you'd say that when we grabbed each
other's hands in a link, we were linked together?"

He did just that with their hands, crossed their fingers
together.

"I know it's not the same as being together forever, but
I will forever be linked to you, as a brother who will always
be here for you."

Then he started humming her favorite Disney song,
'A Whole New World.'

"Remember one of the reasons you were so excited
to go to India? Your favorite Disney movie was 'Aladdin,'
which takes place in India. Your favorite song was this one.
I thought if I could sing you at least part of it that it would
help you gain consciousness. I know that sounds pretty
stupid, but it's something, so here goes.

"'I can show you the world, shining, shimmering, splen-
did,'" he sang. "'Tell me, princess, now when did you last let
your heart decide? I can open your eyes.'"

At this point, Holden's voice broke. He kept singing,
wishing he really could open her eyes.

"'Take you to wonder by wonder. Over, sideways and
under on a magic carpet ride. A whole new world. A new
fantastic point of view. No one to tell us no, or where to
go or say we're only dreaming.'"

Then, something unexpected happened.

Kaia, in a soft, barely audible voice, sang along.

"'A whole new world. A dazzling place I never knew, but when I'm way up here, It's crystal clear that now I'm in a whole new world with you.'"

"Kaia? You're awake? It worked?" Holden said before he got down and his knees and began sobbing.

"Yes, I'm awake." Kaia also said through tears. "I can't believe you're here."

"I'm here," Holden said, crying on Kaia's hand. "I'm so sorry for leaving you," he said as he buried his face in her hand.

"It's okay, you're back now," Kaia said, holding his face with her other hand because he wouldn't let go of the other one.

They sat like that for a while, Holden holding Kaia's hand in both of his, while he knelt on the floor and Kaia was laying down, holding Holden's face with her free hand.

*Chapter 13*

After a week, Kaia was able to go home, to her new home. Holden had made it possible for them to buy it. It was the Davis' old home, the one they had rented before their parents died.

"I can't believe you bought it. We have so many good memories in this house." Kaia said to Holden as he helped her inside.

"I know. That's why we bought it," he said.

Together, both Holden and Kaia went through all the rooms. As they went into Holden's old bedroom, Kaia asked, "Do you remember how we would play house right here with your play kitchen and my baby dolls?"

"Yeah, you were the mom, and I was the dad. I thought that would be a reality someday, but it won't be." Holden said with a sad smile.

Why can't it be?"

"Well, there was a time when I asked you and you said no. Then I disappeared for two years and now you and Finley are together."

"Yes, that may be true, except for that last part."

"What do you mean?" asked Holden, both confused and happy.

"I told Finley that I didn't want to marry him, that I loved someone else," Kaia said, eyeing Holden, more than a little embarrassed.

"Who?" was all Holden could think to say.

"Well, this person has asked me to be his wife before, but it's obvious that I said no. Then, I've had dreams about him since he left me," she said. "Can you guess who now?"

"I want to say it's me, but I don't know."

"What do you mean you don't know? Of course it's you." Kaia said, and she did the high five, linking things with their hands.

"Y-you love me?" Holden said, with tears in his eyes.

"Yes, don't you love me?" Kaia said, who also had tears in her eyes as she cupped her hand on his face.

"Of course I do."

"Then don't you have something to ask me?"

"I do." Bending down on one knee and pulling out the velvet box with his grandmother's ring in it, the ring he had used to ask Kaia to marry him so long ago. "Kaia Kelly, the love of my life, will you marry me?" he asked.

"Of course," Kaia said as she wrapped her arms around him and kissed him, a kiss they had both been waiting for.

"Wait, what dreams did you have about me?" Holden asked once they were hugging again.

"Well, you'd call my name over and over again. I would try to find you, and then I'd turn around and see you there. You would say, 'Kaia! I can't believe it's you! I can't believe I found you!' and 'Please, Let's never be separated again, I love you, Kaia. I love you with all my heart.' Then I would

say, 'I love you too,' and just as we were about to kiss you,
I would wake up."

"Wow, I had one like that too, except the opposite.
I love you."

"I love you too." and they kissed again.

"So how did Finley take your 'Sorry, I'm not marrying
you, I love someone else'?" Holden asked.

"He said what he's said lots of times before, that we are
practically siblings and I wasn't being smart at choosing you
over him. So he just reacted like normal."

"I bet."

"Holden, we belong together because we're better
together."

"I like that we are better together," Holden said.


*Epilogue*


Five years later, what Kaia had said that day, "We Belong
Together Because We're Better Together," was typed up and
framed and put in the middle of their new family picture wall.

The wall was always full of pictures, from when Holden
and Kaia were little to now when their family had grown two
people more.

"She's so precious," Eloise said, talking about Holden
and Kaia's little girl.

"Kiana is precious, and she's my little girl," Kaia said.

Leroy, who was now 19 and had started dating Eloise,
turned around as he played with three-year-old Holton.
"I got you!" he said.

"You did. I've just got to be faster next time," Holton
said, "Mama?"

"Yes, my darling?" Kaia answered, looking at her
little boy.

"Can I go play outside with Aunt Eloise?" Holton asked. He loved playing hide-and-go-seek outside with his favorite aunt.

"Yes, and while you're out there, can you tell your dad that it's his turn to change Kiana's diaper?"

"I will. Now come on, Aunt Eloise, Mom said we could go play," Holton said as he pulled her out the door as everyone laughed at his eagerness.

# AFTERWORD

"Turn on the light!" Turn on the light!" That's what I was struggling to scream, in my nightmare—instead it just turned into an unintelligible slur of sounds as I fought against the ropes that bound me to a straight-back chair. My brain could articulate what I wanted to communicate, but my mouth couldn't. After trying, over and over and over, I woke up.

This was just the latest in a number of bad dreams . . . I am not sure what drives them. Maybe it is dismay at the world's political partisanship, or perhaps the fear of the delta variant. It could be much more personal—underlying angst at the transition into retirement, family concerns, the after-effects of adjusting to a new physical regime (less dancing, more weight-lifting). Whatever.

But at least this nightmare didn't leave me silently sobbing, deeply hesitant to go back to sleep.

Instead, I was thinking about the three young writers in this anthology, and how they have learned to "turn on the light" for themselves. Furthermore, they have been willing to share their imaginations with us.

Writing is a most difficult process, and at an early age, they are investing the time and thought this process demands. *Lightly Fantastical*, the book you are holding in your hands, is a direct result of that discipline.

When we started the Winter Sports session on book-publishing at Teton Middle School, we vaguely thought that if there were enough students, we might actually publish a book. It would be a challenge, with only four sessions of meeting together. And with only two kids participating that first day, it seemed less likely.

When McKelle joined us on the second week, this trio gave us optimism that this idea COULD become a reality.

Throughout that month, and in a couple extra sessions, the interest these girls exhibited in doing so went beyond our expectations.

They talked about what kinds of books they liked, what series they reread, often over and over again, and the volumes they already had bookshelves at home. We shared about the history of printing and the art of letterpress; the Idaho Public Television video about Rick and Rosemary Ardinger, our friends at Limberlost Press in Boise, brought this lesson to life.

They learned about the parts of a book, and we examined all kinds of them. We folded, cut, and created a simple octavo ourselves. They read some of their pieces aloud; Peter read the opening chapter of his book *Follower*.

Peter compiled a slideshow of images of great libraries from around the world. We shared this while sitting in the Anderson library at our home north of Driggs. There, among the books we've personally collected over six-plus decades (and more, from family treasures), Peter and I showed these youngsters that books aren't just something you own. Rather they can play an integral part of life; they certainly do in our life together.

Most importantly, they committed to this book, came up with a title, a publishing-house name, crafted biographical notes, and wrote two pieces each.

The words here are theirs, as are the plotlines. Editing has been minor (fixing typos and such) and we are grateful for the design assistance of Meggan Laxalt Mackey of Studio M Publications & Design in Boise for the final product's design and professionalism.

Lastly, having worked on a large number of community publishing efforts, including *Spindrift* (published by the

Teton Arts Council in 2001) and *Teton Valley Recipes Now and Then* (published by the Teton County Museum in 2006), I am proud that three young women from Teton Valley could come together to create *Lightly Fantastical.*

Next time a nightmare disturbs my sleep, thoughts of "turning on the light," in all its meanings, but especially of Avery, McKelle and Jemma, will hopefully ease my mind.

—*Jeanne Anderson*

# CONTRIBUTORS

JEMMA DYER

*I am J.P. (Jemma) Dyer, a 12-year old sixth grader.*
*My parents are (Jonah) Lisa Dyer and Stephen Dyer.*
*I am the younger sister to Huck Dyer and I live in*
*Teton Valley, Idaho. I have two cats, Thumper and Wicket.*
*I love to read, write, and hang out with my friends.*


AVERY MISKIN

*Avery Miskin here. I have several siblings, my dad teaches*
*high school history and my mom helps produce the*
*Distinguished Young Woman competition every spring.*
*I live in a house on a road, and will be a freshman at*
*Teton High School in the fall of 2021.*


McKELLE SNEDAKER

*My name is McKelle Eloise Snedaker. I am 13 years old and*
*have three siblings, an older sister, and two younger broth-*
*ers. I have lived in three different states—Idaho, Illinois, and*
*Texas. My favorite things to do in my spare time are read-*
*ing, writing, and river surfing (the best sport in the world!)*
*My preferred genres to read and write in are historical and*
*realistic fiction with a bit of romance. I have countless favorite*
*authors, but my two favorites are Lucy Maud Montgomery*
*with her Anne of the Island series and Melanie Dickerson*
*with her entire Hagenheim series.*

# ACKNOWLEDGMENTS

First, we appreciate the dedication of these students and their parents.

Thank you to Teton School District 401 for providing the unique learning opportunity of "winter sports." This four-week session allows students to be out of their regular class routine one day each week; besides alpine and cross-country skiing, snow-boarding, and ice-skating, kids can choose from topics on offer that range from swimming to cake decorating—book publishing was presented for the first time this year.

Members of the administration who provided assistance include Superintendent of Schools Monte Woolstenhulme and Teton Middle School principal Brian Ashton, along with Trudy Treasure and Tricia Taylor who efficiently run the TMS office. They helped with parent contacts, especially for the field trip to our library, answering questions, and such. Special shout-out to TMS teacher Natasha Peterson, who allowed us to use her classroom for our meetings.

Another special nod to book designer Meggan Laxalt Mackey of Studio M Publications & Design in Boise, who provided professional advice to create this final product.

Lastly, we acknowledge each other's work—organizing class content, copy editing, finding art, and in general, just hanging in there.

*—Peter and Jeanne Anderson*
*Teton Valley, Idaho*

# COLOPHON

*Lightly Fantastical* is an anthology of young writers who have the potential to grow talents that will help them forge new creative pathways of the future. They learned that the art of writing requires dedication to one's craft. Also, these students learned that creative endeavors, such as producing a book, depend on community for inspiration and support.

The book cover, page design, and typography intentionally represent growth, creativity, and community. The *Lightly Fantastical* cover is vibrant, just like the three authors. The tree graphic merges realistic leaves and limbs with digital, computer-chip extensions—not unlike the world these students navigate today. The image of the tree, though, stands analogous to what we hope for our youth: strong roots, healthy growth, and solid limbs that will help enable them to reach to their full potential.

The headlines are set in "P22 Arts & Crafts," by the P22 Type Foundry. This font is a tribute to the Roycrofters, a community of young artisans who influenced early 20th century design known as the American Arts and Crafts movement. A member, type designer William Joseph "Dard" Hunter (1883-1966), was a budding artist who forged new designs for the Roycroft community.

Contemporary book designers rely heavily on Adobe Systems, a company that was started by young designers that grew to transform digital typography worldwide. *Lightly Fantastical* body copy is set in "Minion," a serif typeface designed by Robert Slimbach in 1990. Minion was inspired by classic late Renaissance-era type, intended for book and other print use. Minion is a nod to new typefaces created by the digital design community: it's included in the Adobe Originals collection of serif typefaces that are created specifically for books and fine printing.

HOUSE ON A ROAD BOOKS
TETON VALLEY — IDAHO

2021